The vial shattered, oozing its greasy contents all over the floor. Either the woman following Pias did not notice the stain in time or else she could not stop in time, because she hit the slippery spot at full speed. Her feet went out from under her, and she slid diagonally down the hallway, crashing into the lefthand wall with a solid jolt that made Yvette wince. Then Pias had reached her, and stretched out his hand to grasp hers. 'Let's get out of here,' he gasped, pulling her along with him. Yvette was forced to agree; now that their presence had been discovered, it was only a matter of seconds before even more security forces were alerted. And besides, she didn't want to face that woman in battle even more than Pias did . . .

The Purity Plot is the sixth novel in the pulsating interplanetary series featuring the Family d'Alembert – all in Panther Science Fiction.

Also by E. E. 'Doc' Smith

The Lensman Series
Triplanetary
First Lensman
Second Stage Lensman
Grey Lensman
Children of the Lens
Galactic Patrol
Masters of the Vortex

The Skylark Series
The Skylark of Space
Skylark Three
Skylark of Valeron
Skylark DuQuesne

The Family d'Alembert Series (with Stephen Goldin)
The Imperial Stars
Stranglers' Moon
The Clockwork Traitor
Getaway World
The Bloodstar Conspiracy

Other novels
Spacehounds of IPC
The Galaxy Primes
Subspace Explorers

E. E. 'Doc' Smith
with Stephen Goldin

The Purity Plot

Volume 6 in *The Family d'Alembert* Series

PANTHER
GRANADA PUBLISHING
London Toronto Sydney New York

Published by Granada Publishing Limited
in Panther Books 1978

ISBN 0 586 04339 X

A Panther UK Original
Copyright © Verna Smith Trestail 1978

Granada Publishing Limited
Frogmore, St Albans, Herts AL2 2NF
and
3 Upper James Street, London W1R 4BP
1221 Avenue of the Americas, New York, NY 10020, USA
117 York Street, Sydney, NSW 2000, Australia
100 Skyway Avenue, Toronto, Ontario, Canada M9W 3A6
110 Northpark Centre, 2193 Johannesburg, South Africa
CML Centre, Queen & Wyndham, Auckland 1, New Zealand

Made and printed in Great Britain by
Cox & Wyman Ltd
London, Reading and Fakenham
Set in Linotype Pilgrim

Dedicated to the Levin crew: Leon, Sylvia, Barbara, Jeffrey,
Elliott – and, by marriage, Alan and Dru.

S.G.

CHAPTER ONE

THE GLASSEYE GANG

The planet Glasseye was named for its appearance from space. Tuan Ho, the scoutship pilot who discovered it, remembered his initial impression in an interview with *Imperial Newsworks Reelzine*: 'I came out of subspace and there it was staring straight at me – a large blue-green ball with that one dark continent in the center. It looked for all the universe like a glass eye being displayed on a piece of black velvet, with the stars as a background to lend effect to the scene.'

Since that discovery in 2374, the planet had been well explored and colonized, and its name took on an extra significance. The one major continent was found to contain rich deposits of a fine silicate mineral – called fargerite, after its discoverer – that occurred nowhere else in the Galaxy and, furthermore, this silicate produced some of the finest glass ever made. 'Glasseye glass' became renowned throughout the Empire, and no one with any pretensions to culture would feel his collection of *objets d'art* complete without several pieces. Producing, blowing and exporting the glass became the leading industries, and the entire world thrived, basking in the glow of its reputation.

So abundant was the fargerite that the Glasseyers even used it as a construction material for building their cities. When combined and fired in the proper way, it became a substance stronger than steel, with the added advantage that it was more easily recyclable. If one tired of it in one form, it could be melted down and reshaped into something else with a minimum of trouble.

Glasseye cities therefore looked like fairy towers of crystalline perfection. Glass needles rose into the sky, their walls refracting the sunlight into a million rainbow patterns. Glass latticeworks connected the city into a transportation system of small highspeed shuttles that whisked people wherever they chose to go in a matter of minutes. The cities presented an ever-changing face, as old portions were constantly being melted down and replaced with newer, more modern looking sections. Transience became engrained into the planetary character of the Glasseyers themselves; there was a joke common throughout the Empire about a starving Glasseyer who was given a bowl of apples, pears and grapes, but died before he ate any – he was not quite satisfied with the arrangement of the fruit in the bowl!

Visitors flocked to Glasseye from all over the Galaxy to observe the breathtaking beauty of Glasseyer cities. Tourism was Glasseye's second largest industry; the planet represented an almost perfect visual paradise.

But even Paradise has its problems.

The group of masked figures had little trouble breaking into the new Imperial Trade Tower in Southbeach City. This tower, the latest in a series of new buildings to house the local arm of imperial administration, was not scheduled to open officially for another week, while final checks of the wiring and plumbing were completed. There were only two guards stationed at the building's base, and they hadn't been expecting any trouble. The party of invaders blasted them in cold blood, then continued on with their mission.

The leader checked the elevator tube and found it in workable condition. He and his friends got in and rose quickly to the upper stories. The Imperial Trade Tower had been designed like an enormous tulip about to blossom, with the bulb beginning a full thirty stories above ground level. The intruders got off at the thirty-fourth floor and spread out. Each of the eight team members planted his explosive charge in one of the offices around the floor's perimeter, then returned to the central shaft. They went up the tube four more floors. So far, everything had gone according to their plans, but now they ran into something they had not counted on: people.

As it happened, this brand new building, a showcase of Glasseyer architecture and design, had attracted the interest of Lord Hok Fu-Choy, nephew of Grand Duke T'Chen who owned Sector Seventeen in which Glasseye was located. Lord Hok had requested a personal inspection while he was here on Glasseye, and Baron William of Southbeach was most happy to consent. During the day, though, the building was still swarming with construction workers, and it would be hard for Lord Hok to observe it in its proper form. Also, the Baron promised, he would get a splendid nighttime view of the panorama of Southbeach City if he came up here after hours. Lord Hok agreed to a nighttime tour.

Neither Baron William nor his guest had expected to encounter any trouble in an uncompleted building during an unannounced visit. Each man only had one escort/bodyguard with him – wholly inadequate, it turned out for the situation they found themselves facing.

It would have been hard to say which side was more surprised at seeing the other there, but the invaders – who'd been keyed up for anything that might happen – recovered first. Being well armed, they drew their guns to kill the strangers – and they would have, but the leader recognized the Baron and Lord Hok. Making a snap decision, he ordered his followers to take them alive.

The escorts fought well, and managed to burn down two of their attackers, but they were hopelessly outnumbered. In the end, they lay dead on the floor while the two noblemen looked on, helpless. The saboteurs took their prisoners and set the remainder of their explosive charges. Then, herding their captives into the elevator tubes, they descended once more to the ground level and to the shuttle prepared for their escape.

They pushed Lord Hok into the craft first. The young nobleman resented this brusque treatment and, despite the guns that were trained on him, he began a brief struggle. His attempt did not last long, as one of his captors hit him soundly across the face with the butt of his blaster, but the minor scuffle did give Baron William a chance to break free of the men who were holding him. Before any of the invaders knew quite what had happened, the Baron was running down the transit tube into the darkness. A couple of the men started after him, but they were called back by their leader. Their time was running out; they dared not waste any by chasing the fleeing man. They still had one captive, after all, and a very important one at that. Headquarters would approve highly of what they'd done; there was no need to endanger themselves further.

The shuttle with the six surviving invaders and their hostage sped away from the Imperial Trade Tower at top speed. Baron William arrived back at the scene ten minutes later, accompanied by a squad of police, but by that time it was too late. Within another five minutes, the 'bulb' of the tower blew apart, scattering shards of glass for kilometers in all directions.

The Head of the Service of the Empire was greatly disturbed by this latest incident of anti-imperialist terrorism. His organization was charged with the awesome task of maintaining the security of an empire that was spread out over more than thirteen hundred worlds – and that job, never an easy one under the best of circumstances, had only been getting harder of late.

Maybe I'm starting to feel my age, he thought, *but the last two years have really been downhill.*

Not that Zander von Wilmenhorst was that old; at just under fifty he was only now reaching the absolute prime of his mental capacities. But the responsibility of his position would age anyone quickly – and the more dedicated he was, the more seriously he took his duties, which only exaggerated the problem.

He had thought, many months ago, that the breakup of Banion's well organized plot against the Empire would be the peak of his career, that everything following it would be an anticlimax. To some extent that was true, but it was not the way he had expected. Little things kept popping up – almost trivial in and of themselves, but they had a habit of taking unexpectedly large bites of the Service's time and energy. He had fought off the wolf named Banion – mostly through the talents of his two most capable agents – but now he found the Empire plagued by mosquitoes. And he could not help but recall that it was mosquitoes that carried the germs of malaria.

Acts of terrorism were on the increase. The seeds of discontent were sprouting on planets in every sector of the Empire, with a violence unexpectedly strong considering the

8

mild and peaceful reign of Emperor Stanley Ten. Everywhere, groups of malcontents were springing up, chanting slogans for the abolition of the Empire and the destruction of the nobility. For the most part the groups were led by honest, sincere people who believed in autonomy for their own planets without regard for the larger picture of interstellar relations.

Von Wilmenhorst could not fault the people for their sincere, if misguided, patriotism; the simple fact of the matter was that a strong central concept such as the Empire of Earth was necessary to prevent countless interplanetary wars between rival worlds, and the deaths of untold trillions of human beings.

The localized insurrections themselves bothered him little if at all; they were on a scale that the planetary authorities could reasonably handle. But his shrewd mind detected a pattern behind the sudden rise in these problems – and patterns were what he was most suspicious of.

There's a pattern behind every major movement in the Galaxy, he thought. *Find the pattern and you're halfway to finding the solution.*

He had on his desk a series of charts, correlating the growth of terrorist movements. If this had been a medical situation, he would have called it an epidemic. So far, six hundred and forty-seven worlds had anti-imperial terrorist gangs of serious strength, and there was no telling how many more were in the process of formation as he sat here and considered the problem. It would be more understandable if Stanley Ten were a harsh, tyrannical ruler as some of his predecessors had been; people had a natural tendency, after a while, to rebel against such oppression. But on the contrary, Stanley Ten's reign had been one of the most enlightened since the Empire was formed – and, after forty-six years, would soon be coming to a close anyway. While it was not generally known, Stanley Ten planned to abdicate in six months in favour of his daughter Edna . . .

With that thought, a major piece of the jigsaw puzzle fell into place in his mind. Stanley Ten was not the target. Whoever was masterminding this operation was biding his time, building his power slowly, sapping the Empire's strength with a million tiny brushfires. The real conflagration would come during the changeover, when everyone was in a natural state of confusion anyway. The Empire would be in the hands of a young woman who, while possessing many of the strengths that so characterized her father, was not as experienced as he at dealing with crises. There was more possibility that she, through simple inexperience, would make the fatal slip that would bring about the downfall of the Stanley reign, and possibly of the entire Empire.

With the concept of nefarious conspiracies, his thoughts naturally turned to Lady A, the mysterious woman who seemed to be lurking behind so many of them. She had managed to infiltrate the Service itself, and von Wilmenhorst still did not know how. She was a guiding force behind the insidious humanoid robots, two of which had already come too close to wreaking their havoc on the Empire. She'd managed the planet Sanctuary, building up a constituency of the best criminal talent in the Galaxy. She was involved with an organization of space pirates, constructing a space fleet for purposes unknown. And she'd come within a hair's breadth of pulling off the Galaxy's most daring coup at the wedding of Crown Princess Edna.

All of her plans, with the exception of the leak from within the Service itself, had been thwarted by the timely actions of his agents, but that did not make the Head feel any more secure. *We've stopped all of her plans that we* know *about*, he corrected himself. *How many more machinations are developing that we may not discover until too late? Lady A is a very busy woman.*

Along with the incidents of terrorism, space piracy had also been on the rise in the last year or so; Lady A had already demonstrated one connection with that, and there might be others. Somewhere, there had to be a weapons stockpile, some central source supplying these various groups with the arms they needed to conduct their battles. Somewhere, two more — at least — of those deadly robots were engaged in their missions of undermining the Empire. Somewhere, lurking even farther in the background, was the person known only as C, the still more enigmatic partner of the mysterious Lady A. Somewhere ...

Zander von Wilmenhorst ran a hand in frustration over

his smooth-shaven scalp. There were mysteries within mysteries, and so little time to unravel them all. His insight that events would culminate at the coronation of Edna as Empress Stanley Eleven gave him a target date to shoot for – but it was so soon, and the enemy had the natural advantage of knowing his plans as well as its own.

Somewhere, a clock was ticking off the seconds left to the Empire – and unless he could think of something, those seconds would be pitifully few in number.

With a massive effort of will, the Head pushed those thoughts to the back of his mind. Despite the fact of the larger plots against the Throne, there were still the everyday details of imperial security that needed tending – prime among which, at present, was the kidnapping of Lord Hok by the rebels on Glasseye.

Turning on his own private subcom set, he punched in the secret identity number that was known to only a few select people in the entire Galaxy. Within just a few minutes, a face appeared within the three dimensional communicator screen – the face of von Wilmenhorst's old friend, Duke Etienne d'Alembert.

Etienne was obviously glad to see his comrade, but at the same time his expression was one of serious concern. The Head of SOTE rarely had the time to make purely social calls, particularly to the secret subcom number. There was bound to be trouble somewhere. 'Bonjour, mon ami,' he said. 'What's the problem?'

Briefly, the Head explained the circumstances surrounding the capture of Lord Hok by terrorists on Glasseye the previous night. 'It doesn't appear to have been a planned event,' he said, 'but you can bet the rebels will make use of it nonetheless. We're expecting a list of demands momentarily.'

'All of them impossible, no doubt.'

'Even if they only asked twenty kopeks, the price would be too high. It would be a signal to the entire Galaxy for a new escalation in these terrorist attacks. I'm already certain there's an Empire-wide conspiracy linking them all together; if this kidnapping tactic, accidental though it was this first time, should succeed, no noble or political official will ever be safe. We've got to crush this threat so thoroughly, and with such determination, that it won't be tried again.'

Etienne d'Alembert nodded. 'And that, I suppose, is where the Circus comes in?'

'Exactly. Ordinarily I would consider something like this inside the jurisdiction of local police officials, with the Service sending along a liaison officer as an observer. But Grand Duke T'Chen is as cantankerous as ever, and he's been screaming for SOTE to get his nephew out of there. As a grand duke he is entitled to such considerations. Also, as I said, I want to make an example of this for the rest of the terrorists to note, so I want to unleash my top weapon at them: you and your family.'

Duke Etienne smiled at the compliment. 'How thorough an example should I create?'

The Head returned the smile. 'Lord Hok must be returned to his uncle alive and as unharmed as the rebels have left him. Anything beyond that, I'll leave to your own discretion.'

'Ah. I am nothing if not discreet.' The Duke's smile broadened into a positively carnivorous expression. 'I suppose, though, it would be prudent to leave a few of the scum in a condition to answer further questions.'

'Yes, please.'

'Time will be a bit of a problem. I'm on Dorlan at the moment. Even breaking off our next three days' engagements and altering our schedule, it would still take us about five days to reach Glasseye – and once we're there, it'll take a little time to develop our battle plans.'

Von Wilmenhorst nodded. 'I know. I've instructed our local chief to stall, play along with them, pretend to consider their demands until he hears from you. He knows he's to give you his fullest cooperation once you arrive, so you should have no problems. And I'll beam you further reports on the situation as it develops while you're en route.'

'We're on our way,' Duke Etienne said curtly, and the screen on the subcom set went blank as he broke the connection. The Head smiled confidently. It felt good to be able to do something positive, and handing a problem to a d'Alembert was as good as solving it.

He turned back to the stacks of material cluttering his desk in neat piles with varying degrees of urgency. Unfortunately, the 'very urgent' pile was still entirely too high for his liking. With a sigh, he reached for the next report from the top of that stack.

It happened to be a summary of the situation on the planet Purity, reported by Marask Kantana, one of his ablest aides. As he read, it became increasingly clear to him that his need for d'Alembert help was far from over.

CHAPTER TWO

THE SILENT SORTIE

The Circus of the Galaxy was one of the Empire's top attractions wherever it played. Even in an era of sophisticated electronic communications, there was something so elemental about the Circus's appeal that it always drew vast throngs to its performances. It was basic entertainment – people executing unbelievable feats with seemingly effortless abandon. Audiences never ceased to marvel at the wonders performed before their eyes.

Duke Etienne d'Alembert, Manager of the Empire's premier attraction, never allowed his acts to be filmed, televised or recorded for sensable shows. In this way, he created an aura of mystery and originality about his troupe that no one else had been able to duplicate. He relied heavily on word-of-mouth advertising to bring the crowds – and he was seldom disappointed at the results.

But there was another, deeper reason why the crafty duke refused all offers to broadcast his show to the multitudes, despite the phenomenal amounts of money offered. The Circus of the Galaxy – meaning, in essence, the Family d'Alembert – was one of SOTE's strongest and most secret weapons. The talents of this remarkable family, all originally from the heavy-grav world of DesPlaines, had been called upon time and again for secret missions much like the one that now took them to Glasseye. Making the faces and names of the d'Alembert clan members easily recognizable by the general public would end their ability to do the Empire's work in secret.

Duke Etienne had long cultivated a reputation for eccentricity. He was likely to cancel the Circus's appearances at a moment's notice to play at some other distant planet halfway across the Empire – and yet, so popular was the Circus that it was always welcome, no matter how strange were the whims of its manager.

Thus, no one was precisely surprised when the Circus abruptly pulled up its stakes from its successful appearance on Dorlan, canceled its last three days, and took off for Glasseye. Dorlan's loss was Glasseye's gain, as far as most of the citizens of either planet ever knew.

Immediately upon landing on Glasseye, while the majority of his people set about their routine tasks of putting the show together, Duke Etienne received a briefing from the planetary chief of SOTE on the situation regarding the kidnappers. Duke Etienne wore a disguise while meeting with the chief, a man named Bergen, so that he could not be positively identified; if Bergen bothered to correlate the arrival of this special agent with the arrival of the Circus on Glasseye, he was discreet enough never to mention it to anyone.

The past four and a half days had been ones of strident demands from the terrorist organization and seemingly abject capitulation on the part of the authorities. Only by looking closely could it be seen that the planetary officials had not given anything away, but were merely stalling for time. The rebels demanded that imperial taxes be distributed to impoverished citizens of Glasseye; very well, said the officials, just give us a little time to convert it into cash. The rebels demanded that imperial military installations be removed from the planet; very well, the officials said, but the movement of so much equipment and personnel required time and involved orders. The rebels demanded that the Empire pay 'reparations' for all the harm it had cost Glasseye during the tyranny; very well, the officials said, it will just take a little time to total up the cost.

The rebels demanded, the officials promised. And always the fulfillment of the promise was just a little way over the horizon.

In the meantime, the local arm of SOTE had been doing some work of its own. One member of the terrorist force, who had been hit and left for dead during the attack on the Imperial Trade Tower, had managed to survive, and was taken to a hospital and given the best medical treatment Glasseye's doctors could provide. His name was Peaks and, the instant the doctors pronounced him fit enough, he was placed under intensive interrogation by the local SOTE experts. Using every trick at their disposal short of nitro-barb – which his system would not have been able to stand – they pried from him all the information he knew about where the gang made its headquarters, how many people were stationed there and what the defensive set-up was like. The local Service officers took no action themselves, though; they waited, as they'd been ordered to do, for the arrival of the special force.

Now that the promised reinforcements had arrived, Bergen had a complete breakdown all prepared. The rebels were camped in a largely uninhabited section of the continent, a dense tropical jungle near a small mountain range. There was only one way into the camp; mountains protected its back and one flank, while a swift-flowing river guarded the other side. The one way in was constantly guarded by foot patrols at irregular intervals. In addition, automatic sensors scanned the area for indications of metal or high energy sources, such as powered blasters. All told, there were better than a hundred people within the camp, and most of them would now be on the alert – they knew SOTE would make some kind of try to get the hostage back, and they would be ready.

Peaks had not been back to the camp since the night of the raid, so he had no way of knowing whether any special precautions had been instituted for the occasion – nor did he know where the prisoner was being kept. The SOTE strategical officers hazarded a guess that Lord Hok might be in the central headquarters hut, but nothing could be said for sure. The attack forces would have to find that out for themselves once they'd penetrated their target.

Etienne thanked Bergen for all his help and advice, then returned to the Circus for a strategy meeting with his brother Marcel. Between them, these two experienced agents came up with what they hoped was a successful plan to smash the rebel base and get the hostage out alive.

The Phase I attack group consisted of ten people. Eight of them were members of the aerialist team that performed death-defying acrobatics under the big tent several times a day. The ninth was Jean d'Alembert, a cocky looking man with a black mustache, long sideburns tinged with gray and a knowing leer on his face. He was the Circus's knife-thrower, and one of its more outspoken, flamboyant members – but, like all the d'Alemberts, he could be counted on in a fight.

The leader of the team was to be Luise deForrest, Duke Etienne's niece, who had done such a superb job of leading an assault group against Rimskor Castle on Kolokov. Luise was one of the Circus's most promising young clowns, and was blessed with an agile body and incisive mind. She had her long black hair tied up in braids for the purposes of this mission and, like the others in the group, she wore a dark forest green jumpsuit to help her blend in better with the jungle foliage around the rebel camp. She carried a small wicker cage strapped to her back; around her waist was a utility belt which, like the belts on the rest of her party, contained various handy nonmetallic tools. They carried nothing that would attract the attention of the metal detectors scanning the entrance to the camp.

The party was driven in large trucks to the approximate area, as close as they dared take motorized vehicles without risking discovery. They were still a good seven kilometres from the camp's reported position.

There they got out of the trucks and mounted a group of trained marponies. These were equine animals from the planet Zachari, smaller, faster, smarter and less temperamental than horses. The dense underbrush hampered the marponies' movements considerably, but they still made good time, and carried their riders to a spot less than a kilometer from the terrorist base in half an hour. The d'Alemberts tied and muzzled their mounts, and continued the rest of the way on their own.

Traveling along the ground would be dangerous here – according to Peaks' information, this area was patroled at irregular intervals, making it impossible to be sure of escaping detection. The whole point of this mission was utter secrecy; if so much as a single warning of their existence were to reach the terrorists, Lord Hok's life would be forfeit.

Therefore, the d'Alemberts scorned the ground and took, instead, to the treetops. In the dim late evening light they scrambled from tree to tree with an agility that would have put monkeys to shame. The density of the jungle was now an asset, because it assured them of adequate holds for getting between the trees. Only on two occasions was there any gap not bridged sufficiently by tree branches; in those cases, ropes were thrown across the gulf and used as high wires. Not once during the passage did a d'Alembert foot touch the ground.

Luise and Jean were less adept at tree-walking than were the other eight, and they slowed the party down a bit. Speed was not the absolute requirement in this mission, however; stealth counted more heavily. The specialized talents of the other two would come in useful later, and their more agile relatives tolerated their comparative clumsiness.

Three times, guard patrols of from two to five people passed beneath their position. During those moments, the d'Alemberts held perfectly still, waiting for the patrols to move on. They could easily have overpowered the guards if they'd chosen, but Luise decided against that course of action. If even one guard should escape, or merely cry out in alarm, their whole mission would be a failure. Similarly, if any of the patrols were missed by their fellows, the d'Alemberts' job would become much harder. It was better to show restraint now than to regret it later.

After an hour's careful treetop march, they came to the small clearing where the enemy's camp was located. Crude wooden huts had been set up as living quarters for most of the rebels, with one large shack in the central area serving as their planning headquarters. In addition, three large caves had been dug into the sides of the mountains against which the camp was built. These caves, according to Peaks, were used mainly for storing supplies, to keep them dry from the periodic heavy rains.

Luise had a choice. The local SOTE chief thought it most probable that Lord Hok was being kept in the central headquarters building; but Luise could not completely rule out the possibility that the young nobleman was being housed in one of the caves, which would be more easily guarded. There were two people stationed in front of each of the caves, while six surrounded the headquarters building. There was no easy way to make the choice.

After a moment's consideration Luise decided to investigate the caves first because they would, in some ways, be the easiest to check. She whispered her plans to her colleagues, and the group moved around the perimeter of the camp through the trees to the point closest to the cave entrances.

At this point, the mission's success rested with Jean d'Alembert. At the knifethrower, he was the only one of the group to bring along any large supply of weapons. A few of the knives he had were plastic, but most were hastily improvised wooden ones. They were all, however, extremely sharp.

His task would not be an easy one. He had six targets, six guards at the cave entrances. The nearest were five meters away, the farthest almost twenty-five. He had to put each one out of commission without allowing any of them to make a noise – which meant a knife to the throat of each one, in rapid succession. It was now early evening, with only the light from various campfires to illuminate his targets. The knives he would be throwing were not the ones he was used to, and the balance would be a little different. All these were factors he had to allow for.

If Jean d'Alembert was nervous, he did not show it. He was a natural-born showoff, and he was used to having lives riding on the accuracy of his aim: the target models in his act were his own wife, Bernadette, and his children Jacques and Marie. He was not accustomed to missing.

He was now the picture of concentration as he crouched on the tree branch, looking down on the peaceful scene in the camp. One knife was in his right hand, five more held in readiness in his left. With a seemingly effortless flick of his wrist, he released the blade toward its target – and, as part of the same motion, he flipped another blade from his left to his right hand, ready to throw agin. One after another, the knives flashed out from the trees, a smooth operation performed with machine precision. In a matter of five seconds, all six guards lay dead, without a sound to mark their passing but the gentle whoosh of Jean d'Alembert's knives slicing air.

With the sentries out of the way, Luise dropped to the ground, followed by the rest of her group. They approached the first cave cautiously. Jean retrieved his knives from the two sentries who'd been keeping watch here, then led the way inside. Luise was barely half a step behind him. Four of the aerialists accompanied them, while the other four stood guard outside in case of trouble.

There were three more of the rebels sitting around a fire inside the cave, but they barely had time to look up and see the approaching force before the d'Alemberts were upon them. Jean finished two of them off with quick flicks of his knives; Luise got the third by wrapping a cord around his neck and twisting it, garrotte fashion. The rest of the cave merely held crates of provisions for the hundred-person camp. With a shrug, Luise led her team outside to try again.

The other two caves proved to be virtual repeats of the first – a couple of people stationed inside each guarding supplies of various sorts, but no sign of Lord Hok. The initial estimate, then, was probably right. Luise led her team back outside and up into the trees once more. They would try their next attack against the headquarters building.

This time speed *was* a vital factor. It was only a matter of time before the dead cave sentries were discovered, and then the general alarm would be raised. There could be no wasted motions now; Lord Hok must be found and freed immediately.

There were six men stationed around the headquarters shack, some on the opposite side of the building, thus making it impossible for even Jean to get all of them. The rest of the assault team, having waited patiently while their relatives stole the show so far, now had their own chance to get into the act. While Jean eliminated the nearest two guards with his knives, the gymnastic team was flying through the air with a precision that had made them collectively famous throughout the Galaxy. They landed lightly on their feet and continued their motion toward their pre-assigned targets. They outnumbered the remaining guards two to one – which, for d'Alemberts, were laughable odds. They took the sentries out easily – and again, they were so efficient that there was no sound to alert the camp. Luise took a deep breath. It had been easy, so far; from this point on, things would move a lot faster.

Knife in hand, she walked boldly up to the door and knocked. 'Who's there?' a voice asked from inside. Luise spoke in a low tone, slurring her words so the person inside could not understand her. 'Just a minute,' the voice said.

Luise could hear the lock rasping, and a moment later the door swung inward just a crack. That was enough for her. She pushed forward against the door, shoving it completely open. The man who'd opened it was pushed backward, a startled expression on his face. The expression was frozen there permanently as Luise's knife came up under his ribs and he fell, dead, to the floor.

Behind her, Jean also rushed in, knives in hand. As he gave a quick glance around the room and sized up the situation, his blades flashed through the air, and three more of the terrorists lay dead on the floor. And still there had not been enough noise to arouse the concern of anyone in the adjacent rooms.

They could not expect their luck to hold much longer. Taking this building room by room would be an arduous and risky project; instead, they would split up and try to hit the entire building simultaneously. This entry room opened into a hallway that ran the length of the building, with five other rooms further down. The rest of her team entered the shack and, at her whispered command, glided softly down the corridor. When they were all in position, two to each door, Luise signaled and they burst into their target rooms.

The action was short and silent. Once more, surprise had worked in their favor, and they were able to finish off their opponents without any harm to themselves. Lord Hok was found tied to a chair in the third room down. He'd been badly beaten and drugged, but he was alive and had apparently suffered no permanent damage.

Had she the time, Luise would have let out a great sigh of relief. But Lord Hok was in no condition to go swinging through the treetops with them, and they couldn't risk carrying him. Fortunately, Duke Etienne's plans had allowed for such a contingency; rather than going out the way they had come in, Luise inaugurated Phase II of the battle plan.

From the tiny wicker cage strapped to her back, Luise took a small white bird with red speckles. She walked to a window, opened it, and tossed the bird out into the night. The bird, a sporinger, flapped its wings in confusion a couple of times, stretching and exercising them after its long confinement. Then, testing its newfound freedom, it soared upward into the darkened sky. Within seconds it was gone from Luise's view, but she could imagine it with wings outstretched, floating on a convenient updraft, spiraling above the camp in ever-widening circles. The sporinger's keen nose would be sniffing the air, searching for some scent of its mate. Sporingers were animals that mated for life, and their sense of smell was so acute that they were recorded as able to detect their mates at distances of up to fifteen kilometers. Once this sporinger caught wind of its mate, which was back with the rest of the d'Alembert assault team, it would fly directly there, signaling to the others a beginning for Phase II.

With the sporinger gone, there was nothing left for the primary team to do but wait. Luise assigned four of her relatives to stay with Lord Hok, guarding him against any intrusion, while she and the rest of the team spread out through the building in case of trouble.

Five minutes passed, then five more. Outside, the camp was still miraculously quiet. She could hear the sounds of laughter and arguments in the barracks a few dozen meters away, and the occasional voices of people calling to one another across the compound. The d'Alembert luck held; no one had yet discovered the bodies of the guards they had killed on their way in.

Then, however, a new sound began to make itself known, like a sudden strong wind springing up from nowhere. From far away, it suddenly hit the camp like a hurricane, rattling the ramshackle buildings and scattering small loose objects around the clearing. The sky, which had been clear, suddenly darkened as an enormous shape blotted out the stars. Then it seemed as though a three-story building landed on the camp.

In actuality, it was a roc. The name of the giant mythical Arabian bird had been given to these creatures from the planet Bahrein, and it was certainly a title well deserved. The rocs were the largest flying animals ever discovered in the Galaxy, averaging ten meters long with a wingspan of nearly sixty. They were covered with a tough bluish skin, and possessed four sets of talons and a sharp, rending beak that could tear apart even something the size of a rhinoceros without difficulty. They were surprisingly lightweight for their size – only four hundred and fifty kilos – but had been known to carry off prey that was more than half their own weight.

Rocs were rarely seen in captivity. There were only fifty-seven scattered throughout the major zoos in the Empire. The Circus had only acquired this specimen two years ago, after many years of bargaining with the Duke of Bahrein. It had gone immediately into the care of the Circus's prime animal trainer, the petite – for a DesPlainian – Jeanne d'Alembert. The frail-looking eighteen-year-old was totally dwarfed by her charge – and yet, such was her aura of calm and her psychic attunement to animals of all sorts that she had slowly worked even this monstrous creature under her spell. While it was not quite domesticated enough yet to make it part of the show, it was quite able to understand Jeanne's simple commands to fly to a given place and take off again. That was really all they needed in this situation.

None of the Glasseye rebels were at all prepared for this creature out of legend descending upon their camp. Not a one of them had ever seen a live roc before, and even those who had seen pictures did not have the presence of mind to connect the abstract concept with this *thing* they now faced. All they knew was that some monster, bigger than any animal had a right to be, was attacking their camp from out of the nighttime sky. They were not cowards; they would have faced an army of imperial troops without flinching. But this was the stuff of which nightmares are made. Giving no thought at all to their weapons, they began running at top speed away from the roc as it settled gently to land in the center of the clearing.

Taking advantage of the confusion, Luise and her party sped outside, carrying the unconscious Lord Hok with them. Luise waved up at Jeanne, who sat astride the roc's short, stubby neck, then helped strap their charge into the make-shift sling that had been rigged to carry him out of here. The roc was very nervous, first at having so many people screaming and running all around it and then having the d'Alembert party fidgeting with the strange device around its neck. Jeanne was projecting soothing emotions and talking to the roc in gentle tones, but keeping the large creature under control required her fullest concentration. At last, when Lord Hok was safely strapped into his carrying harness, Luise gave the animal trainer the 'all smooth' signal, and Jeanne commanded her mount into the air once more. The roc barely had room to spread its wings fully in the small clearing, but a couple of mighty flaps brought it quickly above treetop level, after which it had much more freedom of motion.

The d'Alembert party left on the ground, strong though they were, were bowled over by the winds left by the roc's takeoff. They waited until the gusts had subsided, then scrambled to their feet and raced for cover back into the headquarters building. Their primary mission had now been accomplished, but the entire battle was far from over.

The incident with the roc, from its first appearance until it disappeared once more into the sky, had taken less than three minutes. Some of the cooler heads among the rebel gang were beginning to realize that something more than just the appearance of a monster might be involved in the events of this evening. Half a dozen of them stopped their outward flight, drew their blasters and fired upward at the retreating form of the roc, but the mammoth creature was far beyond the range of their puny hand-held weapons. The terrroist leaders began rallying their frightened troops, and, within another minute and a half, were able to lead their forces back into the clearing in search of any enemies.

Luise and her party watched tensely from the head-quarters building as the rebels made their cautious approach. The d'Alemberts had come into the camp without any powered weapons so they could get past the security detectors, but they had blasters now – taken from the bodies of the rebels they'd killed earlier. Luise had them hold their fire as long as possible while the enemy slowly advanced. She knew there would be doubt in the opponents' minds about a great number of things, and letting them advance in silence into the darkness would only increase their fears. She was not worried about defending her position; the terrorists had designed their headquarters building for the ability to withstand enemy assaults, and Luise's people were all crack shots. They should have no trouble fighting off an attack, if it came to that. But reinforcements were on the way.

With Lord Hok now safely in their hands, there was no need for delicacy, and Duke Etienne relished the opportunity to flex his metaphorical muscles. The instant the roc had touched down at home base, the Circus's Manager gave the order to begin Phase III, the full-scale assault. Armored trucks filled with d'Alembert fighters surged ahead through the jungle, heedless of any alarms they might be setting off in the process. Anyone who got in their way was mowed down mercilessly – as the terrorists had been doing for some time to innocent civilians on Glasseye.

As alarms began sounding throughout the camp, the re-entering rebels stopped and turned back toward the entrance, prepared to face this new, unexpected enemy. Luise waited until the first of the trucks made its appearance, then ordered her own group to commence firing from inside the headquarters building. Caught in an unexpected crossfire, the rebel troops never had a chance. Energy beams began sizzling the night air, and within thirty seconds the terrorist forces were decimated. The few survivors of that fiery debacle broke from the ranks and fled for cover into the dense jungle. Special details were assigned the job of tracking them down.

So successful was the mission that in the end, out of a total of one hundred and three rebels known to be staying at the camp, only six were left unaccounted for – and those were of no significance at all.

CHAPTER THREE

THE IMPERIAL COUNCIL

The Imperial Council was perhaps the most anachronistic element of the entire governmental structure, a throwback to the times before the rigid class system had set into the minds of people through the Galaxy. Unlike the Chamber of Thirty-Six, where the grand dukes met to consider matters placed within their jurisdiction by the Emperor, or the College of Dukes where the rulers of individual planets met to discuss policies, the Imperial Council's constituency was neither fixed nor composed exclusively of nobility. The Emperor appointed its members from among the most eminent people of his time, regardless of rank; even commoners had served in it with distinction, up to and including the exalted post of Prime Councilor. Depending on the ruler, the Imperial Council could be composed entirely of sycophants, cronies, mistresses and charlatans; but a wise and able emperor used his prerogative to appoint people of intelligence and diverse opinions, so that he might better understand all sides of an issue before deciding. The Emperor's word was law, but that did not stop him from listening to advice.

Under Stanley Ten, the Imperial Council had always been a center for lively debate, even on unimportant issues. But today, the issue before it was the spread of terrorism throughout the Empire, and emotions ran strong. As the Head of SOTE, Zander von Wilmenhorst was automatically a member of the Council, and the report he made was mixed. He told the Council of the Service's success on Glasseye, and the news was accepted gratefully by all; but his prognosis for the future set off a bitter fight between the Council's two major factions.

Prime Councilor at the moment was Duke Mosi Burr'uk of Katswabia, a small black man in his late fifties with a smooth shaven skull and gold-rimmed glasses. He looked weak, but appearances were most deceptive; he possessed

26

one of the shrewdest minds in the Empire, and made all his presentations with the force of his dynamic personality. Unfortunately, he and von Wilmenhorst were frequently on opposite sides of any issue.

The P.C. was now holding forth on the subject of the terrorists. 'We cannot continue to let these acts of aggression against the rightful government go unpunished. To do so is to abrogate all our responsibility, to encourage anarchy and to abet rebellion. I applaud the action of SOTE in this particular instance; it proves what I've been saying all along, that fast and uncompromising actions are needed if we're to stop this nonsense. These terrorists smell weakness like a pack of wolves; the only thing they respect is armed force. We have the power at our disposal to obliterate these scum from the face of the Galaxy; I do wish we would choose to exercise it and flex our muscles a little more often.'

Duke Mosi was far from the end of his planned tirade, but his pause here for breath and for dramatic effect gave the Head an opportunity to interject some remarks of his own.

'Having the power, my dear Mosi, implies the responsibility to use it wisely. In some cases, the more power you have, the less ability you have to act. The Emperor's power is absolute, so he therefore must show more restraint than is ordinarily expected. He has the power, for instance, to condemn children to death merely for stealing a piece of candy from a store. But doing so would represent foolhardiness in the extreme.'

'We're not talking about pieces of candy.'These are terrorists who kill people and blow up buildings. Surely you'll concede the moral difference.'

The Head nodded. 'Yes, of course. But I feel we should leave their capture and punishment – at least on an overt level – to the local authorities, the same as we do for ordinary murderers and arsonists. To give them special treatment would be to offer them the recognition they want; by seeming to ignore them, we are thwarting the achievement of their goals.'

'There is a fundamental difference between terrorists and ordinary criminals,' Duke Mosi insisted. 'These people have

27

as their stated aim the overthrow of the Empire. Your Service is supposed to prevent that.'

'And that is exactly what we're working to do. Not by running after them on a case by case basis every time they blow up a building – that's what the local police are for – but by investigating the root cause of the phenomenon and destroying that. Kill the roots of a plant and the visible part soon withers and dies. That's a job the local police can't handle because the unseen part of this unrest spans interstellar distances – but it's the kind of work SOTE does best.

'The Service is convinced that there is a single conspiratorial group behind most or all of these terrorist organizations. That's where we're concentrating our efforts, and that's where I think we stand the best chance of success.'

The debate raged for more than an hour, with both points of view being rigorously defended and attacked. William Stanley, supreme ruler of the Empire of Earth, sat quietly in his seat, as was his wont, and absorbed all that was being said, speaking only when it was necessary to calm down the more excited of the various speakers or to puncture some pretentious metaphors. His eyes and ears missed nothing that happened within the room, and finally – when it was obvious to everyone that the argument was circling around without any further points to be made – he brought the discussion to a close with observations of his own.

'It seems to me,' he said, 'that cracking down harder on the rebels might be a mistake at this point. At the moment, from all I've been able to determine, these terrorists are a decided minority within the Empire – less than a hundredth of a percentage point of the total population, if SOTE's figures are to be believed. They have little popular support. The overwhelming majority of the populace sees them merely as thugs and troublemakers. That's how I want to keep it.

'If I move in with force against these packs of human *kulyaks*, I automatically vindicate their existence. I provide them with the "imperial oppression" they've been decrying so loudly. I give them the opportunity to shout, "If we're not right, why is he sending his goon squads against us?" It will make martyrs, and people will start wondering whether I really am oppressive. I would only be handing the opposition more new converts.

'I agree with Duke Mosi that action must be taken against these gangs; it must be strong and it must be soon. But I think I prefer Grand Duke Zander's plan of action. We work secretly to undermine the conspiracy. Let them have their little fireworks displays; as long as they don't get out of hand, we can afford it.'

He gave a stern look over to the Head. 'And it's SOTE's job, of course, to make *sure* they don't get out of hand – isn't it?'

'Quite so, Your Majesty,' Zander von Wilmenhorst replied.

The Emperor stood up, and all the Councilors quickly rose to attention. 'Then, gentlemen and ladies, I think this meeting has served its purpose. Thank you all for your ideas and advice. Until next time ...' He gave them leave to depart with a sweep of his hand, then reconsidered a bit. 'Zander, if I could speak with you privately?'

'Of course, Your Majesty.'

The Head followed his ruler into the Emperor's private chambers, where pretenses were dropped and they were just two old friends, Zan and Bill, respectively.

'Those generalized terms you were using are all very well for a council meeting,' the Emperor said, 'but tell me, what in hell are you *really* up to these days?'

The Head explained his intuitive feelings that Lady A and her organization were behind these activities. 'As you pointed out, they have so little popular support that they couldn't keep going unless they had some secret outfit supplying them with money and people. We got some strong leads from the raid on Glasseye. I think we've got enough justification now to put the d'Alembert-Bavol teams onto it. If they can't crack the problem, no one can.'

'I hate the thought of cutting short their honeymoons,' the Emperor said, 'but I agree it's necessary. As pompous a windbag as he is, I think Mosi is right. This is a problem that threatens the stability of the Empire – and, if your hunch is correct, I want it taken care of before Edna ascends the

Throne. God knows, the poor girl will have enough problems to face without having to worry about insurrections, too.'

The Head nodded. After a few more minutes of innocuous chatter, the two men parted and Zander von Wilmenhorst flew back to his headquarters in Miami. Returning to his spacious office, he punched the intercom for his daughter, who was also his chief assistant. 'Helena, put through a scramble call to DesPlaines. We've got some assignments to parcel out.'

CHAPTER FOUR

HONEYMOON ON DESPLAINES

DesPlaines:

An inhospitable lump of rock circling a yellow star at a respectable distance. A critic once defined it as 'the slag-heap of the Universe'. It was a world of sharp, jagged mountain ranges, of small but restless oceans, of turbulent storms that would spring from nowhere and cause their havoc, only to disappear once more as mysteriously as they came. It was a compact world with few earthquakes; all of its material had settled into the densest configuration long ago.

Above all, it was a world where things moved quickly. Because of its superdense composition, the gravitational acceleration of objects falling at its surface was three times as fast as that on Earth. Objects weighed three times their terrestrial value, and fell with speeds that astonished the uninitiated. It was not a planet for weaklings or slowpokes.

There was native life on the planet when the first human settlers came, life that had adapted to these hardy conditions. There were grasses and cereals so tough no terrestrial could chew them; trees so hard that the sharpest Earthly axes failed to make a dent; animals that moved like invisible streaks, with two or more hearts apiece just to keep their 'blood' circulating through their bodies.

Human settlers arrived at DesPlaines in 2018, two years after the tyrannical Communist takeover of Earth. They were primarily of French and North American descent, looking for freedom and a better life. Had they known the hell that awaited them on the planet's surface they might well have kept searching. But their ship was having difficulties and they were tired. They decided to take their chances here, so they landed and began their colonization.

More than half of them died within the first three months. The largest single cause of death was stumbling; when objects fell at three times their accustomed rate, there could be no such thing as a minor accident. Heart failure was a close second as a major killer; the human heart had just not been intended to pump blood for long periods of time against such incredible resistance. As if those two reasons were not enough, there were plenty of other factors acting to reduce the population: bone disorders, women dying in childbirth, exotic diseases and native animal attacks. The local predators saw these slow-moving creatures as an ideal food source, and made vast inroads into the colony's population.

Those who did survive, though, were tough. They were the strongest, fastest and healthiest of the original settlers. They knew they were stranded here for the rest of their lives – taking off from a three gee world in a disabled ship was no easy task – and infant mortality in those first few generations was so high that they were forced into extreme prolificity to keep their numbers up.

The second generation was better able to cope with the conditions on DesPlaines than was the first. They combined whatever genes had made their parents' bones and hearts slightly stronger than those of the people who had perished. They had never known any lesser gravity conditions so, while moving at the necessary speeds put a great tax on their systems, things did not seem too fast for them.

With each succeeding generation, the survivors were slightly tougher, slightly faster, slightly stronger. Sixty-two years after the initial settlement, exploratory ships under the Koslov Dynasty from the once-again capitalistic Earth rediscovered DesPlaines. It is known, by now, that there were enough terrestrial-style planets to go around, and that no one need live under such harsh conditions. The government of Earth offered to help move the DesPlainians to a more hospitable world – but, surprisingly, the DesPlainians refused. Their parents and grandparents had died to build this home for them, and they took a stubborn pride in it. 'DesPlainians,' they boasted, 'can live where no one else would dare.' And so they remained on a planet that was officially listed in the Empire's planetary classifications as 'hostile'.

After a while, they even began to thrive there. DesPlaines was a planet rich in heavy metals and precious stones, for which the rest of humanity always had a need, and DesPlaines' export trade was soon booming. The people, too, were an asset. DesPlainians were in constant demand throughout the rest of space as soldiers, fighters, explorers and bodyguards because of their extraordinary reflexes and superior strength.

Of such stock was the d'Alembert family bred – and, in particular, Yvette d'Alembert Bavol. While she was short, standing 163 centimeters, and at 70 kilos mass was more heavyset than was the terrestrial ideal, there was not a gram of flab to be found anywhere on her body. Being a native of a high-grav world had given her the physique, and being a member of the unique d'Alembert clan had put in an extra conditioning that few people in the Galaxy could match. She and her brother Jules had been the Circus's star aerialists before leaving the show two years ago to become SOTE's prime team of agents.

Her thoughts at the moment, though, were far from any conspiracies threatening the Empire. She was sitting on a blanket on the ground, looking across at her husband of less than a month, Pias Bavol. Like herself, Pias was a native of a high-grav world – Newforest, rather than DesPlaines – with the stereotypical high-grav physique; like her, too, Pias was an agent for the Service of the Empire. But right now Yvette was thinking only about the way the ringlets of Pias's sandy brown hair curled down over the top of his forehead, and the way his light blue eyes took on such a boyish sparkle when the two of them were alone.

Yvette had spent the past few weeks since their arrival on DesPlaines showing her groom the sights of her native world. Today she had suggested a picnic in the *Bois Mercredi* at the north end of the d'Alembert estate; Pias, cheery as ever, agreed. It was late autumn in this hemisphere; DesPlainian trees, instead of dropping their leaves, reabsorbed them back into the branches, retaining the energy in order to survive the bitterly cold winter that was to come.

They were in a thinly wooded section, atop a hill overlooking the ducal estate to the south. To the north rose the majestic Razortooth Mountains, at once exciting and forbidding. Pias was looking out at the grandeur of the scenery, unaware of how intently Yvette was looking at him.

'It's all so beautiful,' he said quietly. 'It makes me feel like composing a poem.'

'Then why don't you?'

'You'd laugh at me.'

'No I wouldn't, I promise.' Yvette made a crossing motion over her heart.

'*Khozosho.*' Pias sat up straight and cleared his throat pompously. 'I call this "Ode to DesPlaines":

> '*The mountains go so very high*
> *As they reach upward to the sky*
> *Like fingers reaching for the night*
> *Except the broken one on the right.*
> *The clouds are shapes that I adore;*
> *They look like bugs squashed on the floor.*
> *In the Twin Lakes of Eastwind my gaze is lost,*
> *They look like eyes just slightly crossed.*
> *The valley down below is . . .*'

But that was as far as he was able to get, as Yvette was hugging her sides and rolling on the blanket in a fit of hysterical giggling. Pias pretended to look hurt. 'You promised you wouldn't laugh,' he said.

It took Yvette several moments to regain even a semblance of her composure. 'I lied,' she answered at last, wiping at the tears with one hand. Then, as Pias made a face, she burst out laughing anew. 'Oh darling, that was perfectly *dreadful.* I don't think I've ever heard worse in my entire life. Even Jules has a better flair for scansion than that.'

Pias sniffed. 'I've been told I have the soul of a true poet.'

'Then you'd better give it back to him before he misses it. I think you'd better stick to the things you're good at.'

'What, for instance?'

In reply, Yvette reached one hand up behind her husband's neck and pulled his head down toward hers. They kissed for almost two minutes. 'That,' said Yvette as they paused for breath, 'is better than a hundred poems.'

'It's nice to know,' Pias, answered, giving her a dozen tiny kisses all over her face and neck, 'that I've found my true niche in life at last. But it is a shame you stopped my poem there – I was just getting to the sexy parts.'

'Heavens! I wouldn't want to stop you from getting to the sexy parts.' But for a while, she kept Pias too busy to think of poetry.

As they lay on their backs, side by side, she suddenly asked, 'What are you thinking about?'

'Oh,' he said casually, 'just how I could murder your brother Robert and his three children so that you could become the next Duchess of DesPlaines and all of this could be ours. Nothing serious.'

'Idiot!' She leaned over and kissed his earlobe, then sighed. 'It has been a nice few weeks, but I'm afraid it's about over. Lady A is still out there, plotting her head off as usual, and very soon now the call is going to come in saying that the Empire needs us.'

'Be that as it may,' Pias told her, 'right now we are just two ordinary people on a picnic, and *I* need you. You know my philosophy – live for the moment, tomorrow will be here soon enough.' And he began kissing her some more.

The tomorrow Yvette was fearing actually came earlier than either of them expected. As they drove back from their picnic, through the massive gray stone walls that surrounded the ducal mansion, Yvette spotted her brother's car parked in the wide courtyard before the front entrance. Yvette frowned. Jules and Vonnie had been staying as guests of Yvonne's father, Baron Ebert Roumenier down in Nouveau Calais. They weren't due back for another couple of days. Smelling trouble, Yvette hurriedly climbed the front stairs and entered the building.

Her sister-in-law, Marchioness Gabrielle, met her inside the door. Gabrielle was slightly older than Yvette, with steel-gray eyes, an aristocratic nose and dark hair streaked delicately with touches of red. 'I'm glad you finally bothered to show up,' she said, traces of annoyance in her voice. 'We've been worried. What have you been doing all this time?'

'Probably the same thing Jules and I were doing six hours ago,' Yvonne d'Alembert said, entering the hallway from the large salon off to one side. 'Probably the same thing you did on your honeymoon, Gabby. I don't think it's changed that much over the years.'

Vonnie greeted her new sister-in-law with a hug and a kiss on the cheek. 'You certainly look like married life agrees with you,' she said.

Yvette looked into Vonnie's almond-shaped eyes and smiled. There was a glow about her brother's wife that lit up the entire room. 'You seem to have a touch of that, yourself.'

'You shouldn't stay out of touch so long,' Gabrielle chided, interrupting the other two women. 'In our business we have to be ready at a moment's notice.'

At the mention of business Yvette stiffened slightly. Just as she'd thought, it was time to end their little idyll here and get back to the serious work of keeping the Empire safe. 'What's happened?' she asked.

'A scramble call came in from Headquarters on Earth five hours ago,' Gabrielle said. 'It was specifically for you and Jules. I told them you'd call back, then contacted Jules. He and Yvonne got here a couple hours ago, and Jules has been barricaded in the com room ever since. He wanted you – alone – to go directly there as soon as you got in.'

'*Merci*. Then I'd better get there, hadn't I?'

Yvette scurried away before the Marchioness could make further reply. She reminded herself that Gabrielle really was basically a nice person, but inclined sometimes to take herself too seriously. She was a d'Alembert by marriage rather than by birth, and carried the additional strain of being the actual co-ruler of DesPlaines (along with her husband Robert) in the absence of Duke Etienne. By suppertime, Gabrielle's annoyance would have burned itself out and she would be her old charming self again.

The d'Alembert ducal mansion, *Felicité*, was, like most buildings on DesPlaines, a one-story affair; it simply was not wise, on a heavy gravity planet, to build tall structures. But being only one story did not mean it lacked grandeur. The mansion was a vast complex of rooms and hallways, covering more than half a hectare of ground. There were thirty rooms, not counting bedrooms or 'freshers, decorated in varying degrees of elegance, depending on the situation; there were a hundred and ten bedrooms, ranging from luxurious to cozy. On the spacious grounds behind the house was an enormous camp area for those incredibly rare occasions when the Circus would take time off from its busy schedule to return to home base and try out new acts or repolish old ones. There was also a set of barracks to house the entire clan when that need arose. *Felicité* may not have been the towering castle that many dukes erected for themselves but, by DesPlainian standards, it was still a fine display of ostentation.

Considering the vast size of the building, it was little wonder it took Yvette a full five minutes to reach the com room. The walk gave her plenty of time to think about what the call might be. The secrecy involved almost guaranteed that it was the Head himself making the call. His identity was known only to a comparative handful within the Empire, and he preferred to keep it that way. Even Pias and Yvonne did not know who was the top man of SOTE. There were times when the secrecy seemed a little silly – after all, Lady A and her cohorts knew his identity perfectly well – but on the whole Yvette approved of the system. After all, there were even fewer people who knew of the Circus's involvement with SOTE – including, she hoped, Lady A.

The door to the com room was locked, but Jules opened it at her knock. Yvette's brother was a year younger than she was, but taller and considerably more massive. 'Come on in,' he said. 'The Head's got some jobs for us.'

The face in the subcom unit's screen brightened as it saw Yvette approach. Spymaster and agent greeted one another as old friends – which, by now, they were – and then got down to business. 'I've already given Jules the details of his and Vonnie's assignment,' the Head told Yvette, 'but I'll recap it just for your information. Then I'll give you your own job. Did you hear about the affair on Glasseye?'

'I'm afraid Pias and I haven't had time for anyone's affairs but our own,' Yvette smiled.

'Well, in brief, your family did a superb job of breaking up a terrorist gang there. As they were mopping up afterwards, though, they came across what I consider an important find. The rebels had a supply cave filled with cases and cases of weaponry and explosives, more than they could possibly have stolen from local sources. In addition, one of the men captured in the raid turned out to be the

37

representative of the arms merchant who's been supplying them with their arms. Under questioning, the man revealed some details indicating that one organization is supplying the weapons to nearly every outlaw group in the Empire.'

Yvette gave a low whistle. 'That must really be big business.'

'I prefer your way of putting it. Your brother came up with the pun that business must be booming.'

Yvette grinned and gave her brother a sidelong glance. 'That's my Julie.'

'But seriously,' the Head continued, 'an operation of such scope indicates an organized conspiracy behind all these supposedly independent terrorist movements. I don't think you'll have to strain your imaginations too far to guess whom I suspect is behind it. Unfortunately, this informant was on the selling end rather than the manufacturing side. He gave us a great deal of useful information about the groups buying the merchandise, but virtually nothing on where his outfit gets the weapons in the first place. All he mentioned was some contacts on the planet Nampur. That will be Jules's and Vonnie's job: finding this arms smuggling ring and smashing it.

'Yvette, your job and Pias's will be a little different, although possibly related. I received a report from Marask Kantana about an army that is building up on Purity. Not a guerilla troupe or a terrorist gang, but an actual military organization drilling for possible combat.'

Yvette knit her brow. 'That hardly sounds like our concern. The law's very clear on that point: only the Emperor has the right to maintain an army and navy, not individual planets. It sounds like a simple situation of sending in the Imperial Marines to wipe them out.'

'You should know by now, my dear, that things are rarely simple – particularly where Purity is concerned. This particular outfit is known as the Army of the Just, and it's being formed by one of the most popular evangelists on the planet, a woman named Tresa Clunard. She isn't preaching against the Empire *per se*, but she says that the Empire is facing the worst period of sin and evil in its history, and her army is to go out and fight these nefarious forces wherever it finds them.

'Obviously, we can't let these crusaders go rampaging through the rest of the Galaxy, no matter how holy they believe their cause is. On the other hand, if we send in troops, it looks like we're trying to stamp them out because of their religious beliefs – which on Purity, would only provoke further nastiness.

'That's why I want you and Pias to go in there. Find out if our friend Lady A has a hand in any of that business. If she does, I want you to get the evidence so we can squash it ruthlessly without appearing to be bigots. If this is just what it looks like, I want you to find some way of derailing them inconspicuously. The less the Service's hand shows in these doings, the better we look. But either way, I don't want the Army of the Just hanging around like a fight about to happen.'

The Head spent another hour giving Yvette a more detailed briefing about the activities on Purity, and promised to 'fax her a copy of Marask Kantana's report immediately. Then he wished them both good luck and broke the connection to return to his other duties.

As their boss's features faded from the screen, brother and sister turned to look at one another. It was Jules who spoke first. 'Well, Evie, it looks like the honeymoons are over.'

CHAPTER FIVE

A FIGURE IN THE DARK

It was agreed by the two pairs of agents that Jules and Vonnie would take the d'Alembert private vessel, *La Comète Cuivré*, to Nampur so that they could get started at once investigating the arms merchants. This was hardly a great concession by the other team; Pias still had not learned to fly a spaceship yet, and Yvette knew only astrogation, not actual piloting. The *Comet* would have been useless to them, anyway. They would get to their destination by slower commercial transportation.

The 'fax of Marask Kantana's report arrived shortly after Jules and Vonnie left on their own assignment. The Bavols pored over it eagerly, searching for anything it might offer to them in the way of a lead. Nothing immediate popped into their minds, though.

They also obtained false identity papers as Cromwell and Vera Hanrahan, citizens of Purity who had been visiting relatives on DesPlaines and were now returning home. For once, they had little worry about disguising their Des-Plainian physiques; Purity was also a heavy-grav world, and its people were quite similar in build to DesPlainians and Newforesters. Yvette was to find, though, that working with Pias would be a far different experience than working with her brother. Jules had been an almost compulsive planner. He didn't believe in starting any job unless he had at least a tentative idea of how he would attack it. Situations frequently forced him to improvise, of course, but he always had the general outline in mind before starting to work.

As they settled into their cabin on the ship that would take them to Purity, Yvette began a discussion of what their tactics would be, just as though she were planning with her brother. To her surprise, she found her husband totally disinterested.

'How should I know what we're going to do on Purity?' he asked. 'I've never even been there. I know very little about the place. Most planets, I agree, are pretty much like Earth in their cultural background and you know what to expect when you get there. Purity is one of the exceptions. I can only imagine how funny it would be if, say, Jules and Vonnie tried to infiltrate society on Newforest, with all our old Gypsy traditions. They'd be spotted as frauds instantly. Purity, from what I understand, is like that, with an entirely separate lifestyle from what we're used to. I'll have to get there, look around and feel out the territory before I decide how best to make our move.'

'Oh? And are we both supposed to wait around for a couple of years while you get acclimatized?'

'Pish tush, my dear, you understimate me. We Gypsies are used to sizing up new situations in a hurry. We even have a saying: "No place is a stranger to the Gypsy soul." Give me a week, two at the most, and I'll be more native than the most rock-ribbed Puritan you've ever met.'

'Do you mind if I devise a plan for myself, then?'

'Whatever makes you feel comfortable. As for me, though, we Gypsies live by our wits. We improvise.'

'I just hope you don't do things by halves. What we *don't* need is half-witted improvisation.'

It would have been easy to interpret Pias's nonchalance as laziness, but such was not the case. Despite his stated confidence that he could absorb Purity's culture through his skin, he had brought with them every bookreel about Purity that he could get his hands on, and he spent hours in their cabin staring silently into the viewer, reading and digesting volumes of information. Frequently he would engage Yvette in long discussions of seemingly esoteric points about the Puritan culture that had nothing whatsoever to do with their assignment; it helped him 'understand the Puritan mentality', he said. By the time their ship landed, Pias Bavol had made himself probably the leading non-Puritan expert on the subject of Purity within two dozen lightyears.

The planet was founded in 2103 by a group of religious dissidents – though others called them 'crackpots' – from DesPlaines who felt that life had become too 'easy' for the settlers on that world. God had meant them to suffer, they said, because only through suffering could they achieve salvation. When the majority of their fellow DesPlainians failed to accept their views, the Puritans picked up and left that planet, hoping to find another even more desolate and forbidding. They succeeded after almost a year of searching, and settled in to devote their lives to suffering.

The world they called Purity was another high-grav world, with the same three-gee acceleration as DesPlaines. It was farther from its sun than DesPlaines was, however, with the result that the climate was far less temperate. Snow covered the ground three-quarters of the year, and the temperature rarely got above twenty-five celsius even at the equator in midsummer. It was truly a world on which to be miserable, and the Puritans elevated their suffering to a fine art.

Every religion has its ascetic sects, and word of Purity's establishment brought converts flocking to it from all over. Critics of the time – and some since – remarked on how kind it was of the Puritans to gather all the fanatics together in one place so that they wouldn't bother everyone else. The religion, which had started out with strong Judaeo-Christian tenets, soon acquired traces of other religions as the beliefs of the newcomers sprouted and took hold. Hindu asceticism mixed in with Sufi beliefs, and a veneer of yoga was superimposed over that, with the result that modern Puritanism could be said to have no one father. There was a strong belief in a wrathful God, in the goodness of suffering and in the virtues of self-discipline.

Immigrants to Purity became fewer, though, as Galactic civilization matured. Virtually all Puritans today were born there without choice in the matter – and some found themselves not at all in tune with the philosophy of the majority. It was an increasingly common phenomenon to find ex-Puritans roaming the Galaxy, usually going to the opposite extreme and becoming devoted hedonists.

The bulk of the Puritans, though, were content to sit back on their self-righteousness and wait for the rest of humanity to go to Hell. It was an event they were expecting momentarily, even though they'd so far been waiting for three and a half centuries.

When their ship landed on Purity, Pias and Yvette dressed themselves in native clothes and prepared to leave. Both wore heavy ecru shirts that itched unbearably, made of the fiber of some native plants; Pias had on dark brown pants, of a different fabric but equally itchy, while Yvette was clad in a plain brown skirt that reached to the floor; and both were shod in thick brown boots made of the toughened leather of some local animal. To enhance the suffering, Puritans eschewed the use of underwear or socks; no coats, cloaks or hoods were worn, either, despite the bitter temperatures. That would have been too 'soft' for Puritan standards.

Inside the terminal, Pias glanced around at the crowds of people dressed similarly to Yvette and himself. Nowhere did he see a smile, a twinkling eye or any sign of human warmth. 'Dullness never goes out of fashion here, does it?' he asked, dismayed despite the fact that he had expected no better after what he'd read.

'You should see them when they aren't all dressed up,' Yvette replied.

They found accommodation easily enough, a small boarding house near the center of God's Will City, the capital of Purity. Their room was small and sparsely furnished; the cracked plaster walls were bare of any adornment except a small stitched sampler in a cracked frame, admonishing them that sacrifice was the road to Heaven. There was one bed just barely wide enough for the two of them, with crisp white sheets and tiny wooden blocks to serve as pillows; a plainly carved bantawood chair; and a small writing desk on which lay, naturally enough, a copy of the Puritan Bible.

Pias sat down hard on the bed and immediately regretted the action. 'Ow!' he exclaimed, rubbing his posterior. 'That bed wasn't made, it was sculpted from the native rock. We might do better sleeping on the floor.'

Yvette sat down more easily on the bed. 'Nonsense. It'll be good for your back.'

'How do we turn on the heat in here?'

Yvette looked around, but could see no sign of a control switch. 'I don't think we're supposed to. It wouldn't be good for our souls if we were comfortable.'

Pias made a face and Yvette laughed. 'Really, darling,' she said, 'one would think you'd never suffered before.'

'I thought I had, until I came here.'

Even the food was not to his liking. The boarding house served only two meals a day, morning and evening. Their dinner that night consisted of a bowl of cold stew and bread. They were permitted all the water they could drink. 'Was that bread meant to be eaten,' Pias complained afterward as they lay together on the bed, 'or is that what they use for throwing at sinners?'

'Nobody ever told you the job of being a secret agent was a glamorous one.'

'I'll have to see what I can do to rectify that,' Pias grumbled, but would not elucidate further.

The SOTE agents spent the next three days learning their way around the city and picking up the Puritan customs. Purity was not an urbanized world; the Puritans felt that being close to nature enabled them to be closer to God, and they had structured their society as a ruralized collection of small farms. Even the largest urban centers, such as God's Will City, had populations of less than five thousand people.

Life dragged by at a slow pace on Purity. Most Puritans thought it decadent, if not outright sinful, to travel in mechanized vehicles; there were some groundcars, aircars and copters available for use by offworlders doing business here, but the vast majority of street traffic was either on foot or in carts drawn by eight-legged local beasts. Shops along the street presented no glittering displays, no fancy advertisements – just the name of the proprietor and the goods sold or services performed.

It was Yvette who first remarked on the pattern of the services offered. By the second day she had noted that approximately one establishment out of every five was concerned with religion in some way – either selling religious articles or, even more prevalent, offering religious counsel or guidance. After Yvette's observation, they paid closer attention to those details and, in the privacy of their room, discussed the matter.

'It seems to be a matter of cultural anxiety,' Pias remarked. 'It's already well known that the Puritans consider themselves better than anyone else in the Galaxy. There may be something in their collective psyche, some compulsion to feel superior to others.'

'And in that case,' Yvette said, picking up on his train of thought, 'they wouldn't necessarily stop at their own borders. Everyone on the planet will be engaged in his own personal battle to be superior to his neighbors.'

Pias nodded. 'Exactly. We have a planet where everyone is straining to be holier than thou.'

' "Straining" is a very apt word. That state of affairs is impossible for any sane person to maintain for very long. Everyone, no matter how sincere their beliefs, no matter how devoted they are to their principles, experiences little moments of doubt now and then; anything else would not be human. But doubt is not allowed on Purity; to let any of it show would be admitting that you were less religious than the people around you, and therefore inferior.'

'Thus,' Pias concluded, 'the religious counselors. I suspect they fulfill the dual role of father-confessor and psychiatrist. They listen to people's doubts and then rationalize them away, explain them and soothe the minds of their clients so that they can once again believe that they are perfectly devout. Every society needs something of the sort, to reconcile people's imperfections to their ideal images of themselves; the more obsessed the society is with perfection, the more reconciliation it will need.' He sighed. 'And this is the most obsessive society I've ever seen.'

The closer they examined life on Purity, the more they observed this principle in action. Technically, Purity was governed under the rules of hereditary aristocracy as set forth in the Stanley Doctrine. But the Puritan religious philosophy taught people that names and titles in this life were meaningless in terms of salvation. As a result, the official nobility of the planet received only lip service, enough to satisfy the demands of the Empire; the people who were truly respected, who had the most political power and who actually ran the world were the religious counselors – the successful ones with large followings, whose teachings were followed and whose advice was quoted most often. They were not preachers, exactly – the Puritans had no formal clergy – but they were the advisors to the nobles and the people who were most often heeded.

For their third night on Purity, the Bavols attended a public 'exhortation' by Tresa Clunard, one of the most powerful counselors on Purity – and, according to Marask Kantana's report, the person responsible for the Army of the Just that they were here to investigate. They both decided it was time they looked upon the face of the enemy, and Tresa Clunard had just returned to God's Will City after a successful speaking tour through the smaller farming communities.

The town meeting hall was packed solid when they showed up, even though they had taken care to arrive half an hour early. Pias and Yvette elbowed their way inside, found standing room against one wall, and waited with the rest for the spectacle to begin. There was a buzzing throughout the auditorium that was the closest thing either of them had seen to excitement since their arrival on Purity. As the lights dimmed, a hush of expectation overtook the crowd.

The first figure out on stage was Elspeth FitzHugh, the counselor's top aide and administrative assistant. FitzHugh opened the proceedings with an invocation, and then passed bowls around, making a short appeal for contributions to the cause. Then, when people's enthusiasm was reaching a peak, she introduced Tresa Clunard.

The stage went completely dark for fifteen seconds, heightening the feeling of anticipation still further. Then slowly a spotlight came on, illuminating the figure standing silently at stage center. Gospozha Clunard was not a young woman – middle to late forties, Yvette would have guessed – but she possessed a quiet self-confidence that radiated to the audience a special kind of beauty all its own. Her long blond hair was fastened into a single braid down her back, extending as far as her waist. She wore a floorlength dark brown robe that was both severe and elegant at the same time.

Clunard was an experienced performer, and had her timing down perfectly. She waited until the spotlight had opened to maximum intensity before she began her exhortation. Bowing her head slightly to the crowd, she finally began to speak.

'Brothers and sisters, I am gratified to look out upon you and see so many worthy faces. When I think of all the evil, sin and corruption that is infesting our Galaxy, I sometimes despair for the future of Mankind; but when I can see the faces of so many good and deserving people like yourselves, I am filled once more with the strength of purpose which God, in His infinite wisdom, has chosen to bestow on me. And I rise up again, my faith renewed a dozenfold.

'For there is evil out there among the worlds, brothers and sisters. There is a sickness stalking the planets. There is degradation, decadence and eternal damnation swallowing up humanity even as we sit here. The enemies of God are many, and their wiles are devious. Their goal is the total damnation of every living human soul – and they are winning, brothers and sisters. They are winning.'

The audience was dead calm despite the intensity of Clunard's speech. To the SOTE team, it seemed as though the listeners were engaged in a contest to see who could avoid reacting for the longest time. Clunard paused for dramatic effect, then continued.

'We remain here in our own enclave of piety and we think that, because we obey the Lord's commandments and live according to His wishes, we are safe from the evil that will overtake the rest of our fellow men. We think that our devotion to the word of God will give us immunity in the holocaust to come. We think our godliness will ensure our salvation, no matter what happens to everyone else.

'Brothers and sisters, we are only fooling ourselves. These conceits are a delusion perpetrated by the very evil we think we are avoiding. When that final battle comes, there will be no sanctuary; the flood will be of such monumental proportions that there will be no safe islands on which to hide. The magnitude of the evil is so great, brothers and sisters, that we will be swallowed up as if we never existed. All our struggles, all our good works will come to naught. God will turn His eyes from us, cast us into the fiery pit of Hell with all the other sinners for our failure in our holy mission to bring His word and His way to the rest of the Galaxy.'

One woman cried out, and drew immediate stares of rebuke from the people around her. She sank lower in her seat, and attention returned to the stage.

'Out there on other worlds, Mankind has abandoned its divine heritage, turned its back on salvation and lost itself,

47

instead, in godless decadence. Machines make the decisions, machines till the farms, machines run the factories and produce all the goods that keep the people in their soft lifestyle. Every day, thousands of souls are being lost to the machines – and as the people get weaker, the machines get stronger.

'By remaining here on Purity and ignoring the rest of Mankind, we are ignoring as well our divine duty to God. We can no longer sit idly by and let the forces of evil devour the Universe. We live in a time for action, and the person who sits on his hands, no matter how pure his heart, no matter how deep his devotion to God, that person is as much a sinner as the vilest indulger in the appetites of the flesh.

'We can no longer deny that we are our brothers' and our sisters' keepers. We must go forth. We must scourge the Empire of sin. We must abandon our safe, sin-free world and carry our battle to the fleshpots of the decadent majority. Only by knowing the enemy face-to-face can we ever hope to achieve the victory that God has intended for us.'

She came to another significant pause, and gave her listeners as well as herself a chance to catch their breath. She knew she had reached an emotional peak, and she would be accelerating on the downhill side from here on.

'I know what you're saying to yourselves right now. You're saying, "I am one and they are many." You're saying, "How can a person like me, the humblest, most sinful creature God ever made, fight against the monstrous forces of evil?" You're saying, "Evil is the trickiest enemy Man ever fought. We have no chance against it on its own territory, we can only hope to fight it within ourselves."

'But I say to you that if you listen to such thoughts, then you are being seduced by one of evil's ablest lieutenants – Despair. Yes, we are few in numbers; yes, we are poor sinners like the souls we are trying to save; yes, the enemy has more weapons, both physical and psychological, than the human mind can comprehend. But we are *not* powerless. We have on our side the greatest force any person could hope to have. We have our belief. We have our faith. We have God. His strength is beyond our imagining, His wisdom surpasses all knowledge. If we keep our cause pure and our faith intact, then God will be with us and we cannot lose.'

At this point she started to move, taking a dozen steps to

her left. The spotlight followed her until she stopped beside a metal bar that was the only prop on the stage. 'There are some among you,' Clunard said, 'for whom words alone are insufficient inducement. You need a demonstration of the powers God can give to those who truly believe, who are filled with faith and love for Him. I do not enjoy resorting to theatrical tricks, but I will use all the methods God puts at my disposal to win new converts to His glorious army.

'I have here a bar of ribadium-reinforced structural steel. The bar is fifty centimeters long, ten centimeters thick and masses about twelve kilograms. To those of you who say that our enemy is too tough, let me offer an example of the power that God may grant His servants.'

Tresa Clunard took the bar between her hands and closed her eyes. Her face took on a look of beatific innocence, an expression of supreme self-confidence. The audience was completely still, waiting in awe for the expected miracle to occur. There was a glow that spread from Clunard's face and hands, a feeling of power that radiated from the stage and over the audience, covering the crowd like a blanket of peace.

All eyes were on the bar. For a moment it seemed to glow with an incandescence that would surely have burned the counselor's hands if it were real. Clunard's wrists were twisting slowly in opposite directions, but her face showed no outward signs of strain. The heavy metal bar was giving way to her pull like a stick of taffy left out in the sun until she had given it a full twist; then, without changing expression, she bent the bar upward into a U-shape. Opening her eyes again and gazing at her handiwork, Clunard tossed the bar aside with a casual gesture. Falling at the three gee acceleration of Purity, the bar hit the heavy wooden floor of the stage with a dull clank that reverberated through the crowded hall.

Yvette watched the act with great interest. As a performer herself, she appreciated a good show, and could not help wondering how it was done. The glow, she assumed, could be managed by any skilled lighting technician, but the bar was another matter. She had relatives who were weightlifters and wrestlers, any of whom were easily capable of such a feat; but all of them massed upwards of a hundred and twenty kilos, and their muscles were so developed that it was impossible to mistake them for anything but what they were. Tresa Clunard, on the other hand, could scarcely have massed more than eighty kilos, if that much – it was hard to tell under the loose robe – and did not look at all muscle-bound. She had not had to strain to twist the bar at her pleasure. If the stunt had not been rigged in some way, she was very impressed with what Tresa Clunard could do. Perhaps a little too impressed; an idea began forming in the back of her mind that she did not like at all.

The audience could not help but gasp at the feat, and Tresa Clunard accepted it quietly, even seemed to expect it as her due. She gazed out over the darkened hall, and it appeared her eyes were making contact with every individual in the room. She looked as though she could measure the exact value of each soul and give change where required.

'That,' she said when her audience had again grown still, 'is a sample of the power that the Lord can invest in one of His children who truly believes in Him and loves Him. With a legion of true believers behind it, can any holy cause possibly fail?'

The counselor continued speaking for another half hour. She identified 'the enemy' as the forces of materialism: wealth, labor-saving machines, the desire for easy living – anything that would concentrate a person's mind on the present life and make him forget his obligations toward the next. She spoke in general terms about gathering the faithful together to fight the corruption throughout the Galaxy. Not once did she ever mention the Army of the Just by name, nor did she say the slightest word about raising arms against the established government. She was much too shrewd for that.

By the time her exhortation was finished, the tension within the hall was a tangible commodity, a violin string stretched taut and ready for bowing. And yet, aside from the general outburst of amazement when the bar was bent, the audience sat through the entire speech in stony silence. *It's like talking to zombies*, Yvette thought, and a chill rose up her spine.

As Clunard finished, the spotlight went out, leaving the auditorium momentarily in darkness. People who hadn't realized they were holding their breath began to breathe again, and there was the slight rustling of people shifting in their seats.

Then the house lights came on again, and Elspeth Fitz-Hugh stood on the stage. She waited patiently for the crowd to regain its composure and made another appeal for donations to the cause. This time as the bowls were passed the rubles flowed like a river during the spring thaw. While the money was being collected, FitzHugh made slightly more direct references to an army being assembled to fight for God's cause, although her remarks were still general enough to avoid charges of treason.

With the closing benediction, the meeting was officially at an end. Not many people left the building, though. A majority surged forward toward the stage, eager to be a part of the magic they had sampled earlier. FitzHugh was mobbed by people anxious to learn how they could do more to personally assist Tresa Clunard's cause and, after a short discussion with Yvette, Pias joined that throng.

At last his turn came, and he spoke directly to the counselor's assistant. 'I made a large contribution to the cause, Sister Elspeth,' he said, 'but I really don't feel that was enough for me to do. I want to become personally involved in Sister Tresa's work.'

'It's God's work,' FitzHugh chided him gently. 'Sister Tresa is merely His instrument for directing it.'

'Yes, of course. My error is inexcusable. Nevertheless, I want personally to combat this menace that threatens the salvation of us all. Do you know of any way I can do that?'

FitzHugh looked him up and down critically. 'There is an organization of people who, like yourself, are dedicated to the Lord's fight. Do you have any references?'

'References?'

'In a closely knit, dedicated organization like this, good intentions are not enough. The applicant must be known and vouched for by at least four other members before he may be permitted to join. Can you meet that qualification?'

Pias's face fell. 'I'm afraid not.'

'Then I'm sorry, but I'll have to refuse you for now. If you'd like to leave your name and address, though, I'll keep it for future reference, in case you can be of help to us later.'

Yvette, meanwhile, went up onto the stage and, with a group of others with similar curiosity, was examining the metal bar Tresa Clunard had bent. It was, as it had been described, a heavy, solid metal construction bar; Yvette, with all her strength, could barely do anything to it, and yet Clunard had handled it effortlessly.

As they left the hall, Yvette discussed the matter with her husband. 'Maybe Clunard's just stronger than she looks,' Pias shrugged.

Yvette snorted. 'I don't consider myself a weakling, yet *I* couldn't do anything like that. There's *got* to be some trick to it.' She smacked one fist against her other palm. 'I'm sure my Uncle Marcel, the magician, could think of a dozen ways to fake it.'

'Perhaps it wasn't faked,' Pias said. 'I did a lot of traveling during those couple of years I was tracking down Rowe Carnery, and I saw a lot of unbelievable things. An un-mitigated faith in something can give a person extra-ordinary abilities.'

'You think God really helped her bend that bar?'

'Maybe, maybe not. But her *belief* in God certainly could have. Faith is a mystery no one's solved yet.'

To change the subject, Pias then explained to Yvette his failure to join the Army of the Just. Yvette nodded. 'I was afraid it might be something like that,' she said. 'They're taking exceptional pains that no one infiltrate their group. On a small, rural planet like this, everyone knows everyone else's business. The true enlistee would probably have no trouble getting the required references; it's only outsiders like ourselves who are suspect. We'll have to go about this from the outside.'

She looked at her husband. 'Have you come up with any brilliant ideas yet?'

'Still working on it.'

'Then do you mind if I suggest one?'

'I listen to you in all things, my love.'

'I want to try breaking into Clunard's offices. There's likely to be something there that will give us a clue about what she's up to, or at least where this army of hers is headquartered. We can't fight them until we know exactly what they're doing and where they are.'

Tresa Clunard, like many of the lesser religious counselors, maintained an office in God's Will City. The scope of her operations, though, was far beyond the modest size of her colleagues. For outward appearances, there was only one storefront bearing her name, no larger than any self-respecting counselor would maintain; but the local branch of SOTE informed the Bavols that Clunard's actual offices occupied all the buildings within that entire city block. When a person became as important as she was, there were administrative difficulties that involved large staffs, even if the counselor were not busy organizing a secret army.

The Bavols waited until three in the morning to make their raid. They would be hampered slightly by the fact that they didn't know the layout of the offices into which they were breaking, but that situation was eased by the fact that the security system within the office complex promised to be very light. While there was some crime on Purity, as everywhere, it was punished with such unrelenting harshness that most Puritans bent on a life of crime chose to go elsewhere. A counselor's offices would not be heavily guarded at all, compared to what Yvette was used to facing.

The Bavols had rented a groundcar, despite the fact that it would make them stand out in the streets; there was never any way of knowing when they might have to make a fast getaway. They parked their vehicle alongside the building and, using a set of grappling hooks, pulled themselves up onto the roof of the one-story complex. Both were dressed all in black, with infrared flashlights and goggles to help them see; each carried a set of tools that would be useful for breaking into locked places, and a stun-gun in case of trouble. They hoped not to have to use the latter; the whole point of this exercise was to obtain information without the enemy knowing it had been obtained.

There was a maintenance duct opening out onto the roof. Although Puritans did not believe in heating or cooling their buildings, they still recognized the practical necessity of having vents to the outside so that the interior air did not get stale and unbreathable. The Bavols started to pry the cover off the duct; it squealed hideously, and Yvette took from her belt a vial of special lubricant to oil the hinges. The cover came off more quietly then, and the agents lowered themselves down inside the building by a carlon rope, which they left in place to help them get out again.

They found themselves in a small janitorial area. Opening the door a crack, Yvette peered out, but could see no signs of any guards in the hallway immediately outside. She and Pias slipped out of their hiding place and split up. There was a lot of ground to cover in this one foray, and they could go over twice as much individually as they could together. They agreed to meet back on the roof in no more than one hour, whether they had found anything or not.

Pias moved from office to office, looking for any sign of a safe. Clunard obviously would not leave incriminating evidence lying in plain view, not while the security about recruiting new members to the army was otherwise so tight. Most of the offices were not locked, and papers were scattered around for anyone to read. He ignored them and continued his search.

On two different occasions he heard the footsteps of approaching guards. The security officers were not expecting trouble, and took few precautions to avoid being heard, making it easy for Pias to avoid them. As he moved deeper into the office complex, he could almost sense his Gypsy ancestors peering over his shoulder and nodding their approval of his methods.

At last he came to an area that seemed to have been made more secure than the previous ones. The doors here were locked, and were wired into simple sound alarms. Pias's training at the Service Academy was still fresh enough that bypassing the alarms and unlocking the doors was a simple procedure requiring only a couple minutes' time; after that, he could enter these private offices at will. He could discover no safes in here either, but the desks were all locked and the tops cleared off. He assumed that the important papers had been locked away for the night, so he began the lengthy task of persuading the drawers open to examine their contents.

His search was still unrewarded as he was rummaging through the fourth of these locked offices. As he was bent over the desk looking for clues, he heard a sound. It was very faint, just the lightest scraping of shoe against floor, but with his senses alert for any sign of trouble it was enough to warn him of another presence. He tossed the papers he'd been reading back into their drawer and closed it silently, locking it as it had been so no one would be able to tell what he'd seen. He straightened up, and his right hand closed on the butt of his stun-gun. This was not just another security guard; the person was moving too carefully, too quietly. It had to be someone who suspected a burglar was already here, and was trying to surprise him.

The scene was not completely dark to him; Pias had his infrared flashlight, which illuminated the office's interior with an eerie light when viewed through the goggles he wore. The problem was, the beam was a narrow one, focusing on a small area. Pias set the flashlight gently down on the desktop facing the door so that its rays would show him anyone who entered; since he was wearing the special goggles and the other person probably was not, he would be the one to benefit. He stood up and backed away a few paces, his stunner aimed directly at the door.

The quiet footsteps outside came right to the edge of the door and then stopped. The doorknob began a slow turn, and Pias's finger tightened over the firing button of his weapon. His heart was pounding so loudly that he thought it would surely alert whoever was out there that the SOTE agent was inside, waiting.

The doorknob stopped turning, and there was a heart-stopping pause that lasted all of two seconds. Then, with unexpected speed, the door flew inward and a figure burst into the room. The invader was a female, but Pias could not tell much more than that; once she was inside the room, the other person dashed out of the flashlight's beam into general darkness of the room.

Pias was astonished. *No one* should be able to move that fast, not on a three-gee world. The idea had occurred in the back of his mind that this might be Yvette, accidentally covering the same ground – but he knew his wife could not move that fast. This woman had burst into the room with a speed comparable to what a heavy-grav native could achieve on a one-gee world – and on Purity, such a feat should be beyond human capacity.

Pias fired his stunner at the intruding form, but he must have been too slow because she did not stop. She moved instead into the shadows out of the beam of his flashlight.

Pias could still see her through his goggles as a humanoid-shaped glow of a heat-emitting source, but there were no fine details such as facial characteristics.

She must have seen him, too, although she didn't appear to be wearing goggles, for as soon as she was out of the direct beam from the flashlight she started toward Pias at the same incredible speed. Pias turned to face the threat from the slightly different direction, and fired his stunner point-blank into the charging woman. His weapon was set on three, enough to stun a person for about twenty minutes; his attacker should have dropped in her tracks long enough for him to get out of there and warn Yvette that they'd been discovered.

Instead, the woman continued her charge.

Had Pias Bavol been one whit less resourceful, had his mind been duller or his reflexes slower, the only thing left to write about him would be his obituary. But, startled though he was by the stunner's lack of effect, his instincts refused to let him freeze up. The glowing shape was speeding toward him out of the darkness, and he had to get out of its way. He fell slightly to one side, rolling as he'd been taught to avoid injury even under these gravity conditions. In one smooth motion he had evaded the immediate charge and rolled to his feet once more. He had his stunner up and fired again at the figure – and again, to no avail. As the woman turned to come after him again, he threw the gun directly into her face. Without flinching, she reached up a hand to brush the projectile aside.

It was at this point that Pias decided to exercise the better part of his valor. He had never been the sort to make hopeless stands when simple flight offered him a safer way out. Turning away from his attacker, now, he ran for his life. He left the office, slamming the door behind him. That would only slow the woman down for a second, but every second counted.

On the other side of the building, Yvette picked up the slight but unmistakable sounds of a fracas. Fearing for her husband's safety, she quickly left the office she was investigating and raced out into the hallway, braced for a fight. She stood quietly for a moment to get her directional bearings, then hurried toward the sounds of the skirmish.

As she turned a corner, she ran straight into a pair of guards. Like her, they had heard the strange noises and were on their way to investigate. Being also natives of a three-gee world, they could react with nearly the same lightning speed as she could. But Yvette's training with the Circus, and the fact that she was more prepared for guards than they were for her, enabled her to recover from the surprise slightly faster. She shot the first guard point-blank with a number three stunner beam, and he obligingly collapsed on the floor.

That gave the second man the added instant he needed to recover. As Yvette turned to shoot him, he brought his arm up suddenly, deflecting her aim and knocking the weapon from her grasp. Now that her hand was free of its gun, she used it to grab the man's arm in the unbreakable grip of a skilled aerialist. Planting her feet, she whirled the man around her and, when she'd built up enough momentum, let go. The man flew against the far wall and crashed to the ground; under this gravity, he was likely to have broken several bones. In any event, he was unlikely to cause her further trouble.

Her stunner was somewhere down the darkness of the corridor. Searching for it would use up the precious seconds she might need to help Pias. Trusting to her inborn talents, she ran on in the direction of the noise.

As she turned the corner, she could see the scene clearly. There were two figures running in her direction. The one in front she would have recognized anywhere as her beloved husband. The one following him was some woman whose face she couldn't make out. Pias had no gun; he must have lost it in the fight. But, though the figures were slightly blurry and indistinct in the infrared glow, one fact was abundantly clear – the woman chasing Pias was running faster than any living being had a right to.

Yvette could tell that her husband would not be able to outrun his adversary, and that he did not wish to stand and fight anyone who could move so quickly. She decided to help him along. Reaching into the tool kit on her belt, she took out the tiny vial of lubricating fluid she'd used on the duct cover and threw it with an acrobat's accuracy at a spot just behind Pias, a few paces ahead of his pursuer.

The vial shattered, oozing its greasy contents all over the floor. Either the woman following Pias did not notice the stain or else she could not stop in time, because she hit the slippery spot at full speed. Her feet went out from under her, and she slid diagonally down the hallway, crashing into the lefthand wall with a solid jolt that made Yvette wince.

Then Pias had reached her, and stretched out his hand to grasp hers. 'Let's get out of here,' he gasped, pulling her along with him. Yvette was forced to agree; now that their presence had been discovered, it was only a matter of seconds before even more security forces were alerted. And besides, she didn't want to face that woman in battle any more than Pias did.

Hand in hand, the two agents ran at top speed back to their janitorial closet. Once inside, they jammed boxes and crates against the door to gain them a few extra seconds, then climbed up their rope back to the roof. From there, it was a fast jaunt back to their line, down the side of the building and off to their waiting car. They wasted no time pausing to see whether anyone had followed them out; Pias merely gunned the motor and they shot into the darkness for all they were worth.

Something had gone terribly wrong back inside that complex, and they would have to figure out exactly what it was before they dared take another step near Tresa Clunard's Army of the Just.

CHAPTER SIX

HARASSMENT TACTICS

Unlike Pias and Yvette, Jules and Vonnie d'Alembert had a plan carefully worked out long before they reached their target planet of Nampur.

'The way I see it,' Jules surmised, floating in the cramped cabin of their personal ship, *La Comète Cuivré*, 'the gang we're up against has a virtual monopoly on the arms sales to the underground terrorist organizations. It's the Head's belief that the terrorists themselves are independent groups, but that they're being guided by some central policy maker – and who better to control them than the person who ships them their munitions? They can't function effectively without him.'

Vonnie nodded silently. She still felt a little in awe of her new husband and, while they had both worked together before, this was their first mission as husband and wife. She was more than willing, for the moment, to let Jules do all the planning for the team. She could scarcely go wrong, after all, listening to the ideas of the only man alive who'd received a perfect score on the Service's Thousand Point Test of capability.

'We don't really know who the brains are behind this operation,' Jules continued. 'All the Head could learn was a few contacts on the sales end. We could get in touch with them and try working our way up the ladder to find who's on the top rung. But that's a slow, grinding process at best, and I'm basically lazy. I'd rather make them come to me.'

'By pretending to be a buyer?' Yvonne ventured.

Jules shook his head. 'I considered that, but I didn't like it. Establishing our credentials might be a bit awkward. If we're terrorists, we'll have to do something to prove it – and I have this natural aversion to hurting innocent people. Besides, the buyer never gets to meet the big boss – he deals exclusively through the salesmen. We learned that from the informant we captured on Glasseye. No, if we're going to learn about these arms dealers, we're going to have to be a lot more than mere customers.'

'What, then?'

'Competitors.' And Jules's smile was as broad as a shark's who's just smelled a beach party.

The planet Nampur had little to set it apart from dozens of other reasonably prosperous worlds. Like the planet Chandakha, which Jules had visited once before, Nampur had been settled primarily by Terrans from Asia, particularly the Indian subcontinent. But unlike Chandakha, the entire planet of Nampur was habitable, resulting in less crowding, less crime and less general degradation. The Nampuri were, for the most part, a prosperous and congenial people; the world itself seldom gave the Service of the Empire any cause to suspect trouble might be brewing there. And, as it turned out, it was the quiet worlds that needed watching the most.

There was a man in the city of Lharampas whose name was Panji. According to the Glasseye informant, this Panji was one of the most important distributors in the chain of operations . . . and so Jules chose to make him the target. He and Vonnie broke into the man's home and office, planting microphones in every room and a vidicom set so they could know his most intimate dealings. They followed him everywhere, photographed and traced everyone with whom he came in contact, made and compared extensive notes, until finally – after weeks of study – they knew all the patterns of the man's life. Only when they were sure of their subject did they start to act.

It was little things, at first – vidicom calls late at night which, when answered, showed no one on the other end of the line. Panji would come home to find his front door standing ajar, even though he distinctly remembered locking and bolting it before leaving. Goods were delivered which he'd never ordered. Customers complained that he called them to either make or cancel appointments, and he knew those calls had never been made. Envelopes turned up in his mail containing nothing but ashes. Gradually, though, the pranks escalated. A rock was thrown through his window. Salt was strewn through his garden. A string of dead grass snakes was laid on his doorstep. All four tires were stolen off his ground-car.

Within two weeks, Panji was a nervous wreck. But a man in his position as a major illicit arms dealer could not go to the police to ask for protection against this harassment, lest the authorities pry a little too closely into his activities. Panji therefore went out and hired a squad of professional bodyguards and toughs to watch over his property.

Within twenty-four hours, all the guards had vanished mysteriously, and could not be found anywhere on Nampur. Panji found he could not hire any more – his reputation was preceding him, and no one wanted anything to do with him.

Finally, with the stage well set, Jules and Yvonne moved into Phase II of their plan. It began with a plain, unsigned note left on Panji's living room table: 'Expect a vidicom call.' Panji, desperate to find out who could be at the bottom of this series of tortures, stayed home for the entire next day, glued beside his set. When the suspense had become unbearable, the vidicom rang and Panji answered it with great trepidation.

The visual screen was blank, and all he heard was a hoarse male voice at the other end of the connection. 'There's a yellow wooden bench near a takto tree at the northeast corner of Parrawli Park. Be there tomorrow at two-thirty. Alone.' And the line went dead.

Panji was at the appointed spot precisely at two-thirty. He brought with him an expert marksman who was to hide in the bushes near the spot and pick off whoever contacted Panji; but Vonnie, scouting the area thoroughly for just such a doublecross, found him long before he could cause any trouble. Panji found the man afterwards sleeping off the aftereffects of a sharp blow to the jaw.

Meanwhile, as Panji sat on the designated bench, he found himself approached by a man with a shaved scalp, blue-dyed skin and brown robes of an Arborean mystic. The man sat down beside him and was silent for a moment. Panji wondered whether this was indeed the right man – until suddenly the mystic spoke.

'You and I deal in the same commodity, *tovarishch*,' the stranger said.

'Do we indeed?' Panji, though nervous, still had enough composure to put up a brave front. 'What commodity is that?'

'We provide people the wherewithal to make things go boom, is that not correct?'

'What if it is?'

'Simply this: to date, you have supplied your customers with merchandise from only one firm. My associates and I insist that you start filling your orders with our merchandise instead. We can supply you with everything your former suppliers could, at a competitive price.'

'I've been dealing with this other firm for years. I have a certain amount of goodwill built up. Why should I suddenly switch over to you?'

'We insist *very* strongly,' Jules said. Though his voice was quiet and the words underspoken, Panji had little difficult understanding the implied threat hidden there.

'This is not a decision that can be made easily,' Panji said. 'I've developed a certain loyalty and rapport with my other suppliers. I know I can trust them . . .'

'Rest assured, gospodin, you can trust us, too. You can trust us to be most disappointed if you decline our offer.'

Panji was starting to sweat, though the weather was quite mild. 'I need some time to think it over.'

'Of course. Take all the time you need, up to thirty seconds. Then say yes.'

Jules had not made any movements that were directly threatening, but the implied menace in his voice and the harrowing events of the past several weeks convinced Panji that arguing with this stranger would be less than profitable. He did not know whom or what this stranger represented; until he knew better what he was facing, it would be safest to play along.

'Smooth,' he said aloud. 'What did you have in mind?'

'Word has it that you'll be meeting a customer tomorrow from the planet Wallach. You will fill their order with our merchandise rather than that of your usual supplier. What is their shopping list?'

Now that they were talking straight, cold business, Panji

felt much more at ease. The shrewd merchant facet of his mind took over. 'Two cases of lightweight, PR-3 blasters, a dozen XN-17 heavy duties, fifty kilos of stelemite, one gross acid-mix fuses, seventy-five compression cases. I think that's all. Can you handle that?'

'We could supply that just sweeping the miscellany off our storeroom floor. How much were you going to pay your supplier for providing all that?'

'Thirty thousand rubles.'

'Actually,' Jules said, 'the figure is forty-seven thousand, five hundred.' He smiled at the startled look on Panji's face. 'You see, *tovarishch*, we know a lot more about your dealings than you supposed. Still, we like to give discounts to our new accounts to welcome them into the fold. We can let you have what you need for forty-five thousand.'

'That's reasonable,' Panji nodded.

'Yes, we feel it's most generous, considering you have no choice other than to close your operations down completely.' Jules gave him instructions for meeting tomorrow, promising to have the shipment of arms all ready for delivery. Panji, in turn, promised to bring the required cash payment.

Their transaction accomplished, Jules stood up. 'I know it will be a pleasure doing business with you, Gospodin Panji. I will see you tomorrow. You will wait here until I have completely disappeared from sight, and then you may go about your affairs.' With that, he walked off down the path and was soon lost to view.

Panji was a very worried man. While this newcomer's organization had shown itself to be resourceful at terrorizing one individual, he still had no idea how successful they would be at delivering on their promises – or at protecting him from the wrath of his old suppliers when they learned that he was switching his business to someone else. He knew his old people well, knew what they were capable of, knew that they would stand with him in case of trouble. These newcomers struck him as being ruthless sharks who would cause him nothing but grief. He did not want them to succeed.

Panji found the marksman he'd brought with him unconscious in the bushes, and left him there. It would serve him right for being so careless. Panji could not afford to be sur-rounded by incompetents – not now, with so much trouble brewing.

The stranger could only know so much about his business dealings by tapping Panji's vidicom; therefore the merchant resolved not to use it again for anything crucial. Instead, he went to a public booth and put in a call to George Chactan, the man who always sold him his supplies in the past.

Chactan listened impassively as Panji detailed his recent conversation with the stranger who wanted to take over the business. When Panji was finished, Chactan drummed his fingers on his desktop and stared silently at the screen for a moment. 'You did the right thing coming to me,' he said at last. 'These new people sound pushy. I don't like that. Pushy people have a tendency to attract attention, and that's the last thing any of us needs. There's not that much room in our business for competition. Someone is always likely to get hurt. Your contact sounds to me like an opportunist, a punk who wandered into a situation he doesn't fully under-stand and who thinks he can bluff his way to the top. We can't let him get away with that, can we, Panji?'

'No sir,' the middleman was quick to reply. 'Not at all. That's why I called you as soon as it was safe. This is some-thing I can't deal with on my own, and I need your help.'

Chactan smiled. 'You just relax. Everything will be taken care of. People as obviously uncouth as this man you met should not be handling explosives; they have a tendency to go off unpredictably. Don't bother showing up at that rendezvous tomorrow – I have a feeling our friends are going to be in for a nasty, and decidedly unhealthy, sur-prise.'

The truck was parked precisely where Jules had told Panji it would be, at the large empty loading dock behind a des-erted factory on the outskirts of town. At the hour of the scheduled meeting with Panji, a long black limousine rolled into the lot. As the driver spotted the truck, he gunned the motor and raced toward it, pulling his vehicle into a curve that would come within ten meters of the waiting target. At the closest point of approach, a window opened and a bolt of energy from a high-powered blaster shot out toward the back of the truck. The parked vehicle started burning as the limousine sped away again as fast as the driver could make it go; five seconds later, the truck burst apart with an explosion that rocked the neighborhood for several kilometers around.

Nearly a kilometer above, hovering silently in the sky, Jules and Vonnie were looking calmly down on the scene from their Mark Forty-One Service Special. This extraordinary vehicle, though it looked almost identical to a sports model groundcar, was actually a sophisticated small battle machine, capable of antigravity, jet-powered flight, and possessing an arsenal of all the offensive and defensive armament the Service's technicians could cram into so small a package.

'You were right, Julie,' Yvonne said as their decoy truck blew apart. 'They went for the bait.'

'Of course I'm right. Did you think you married a mere mortal, woman?'

'Even if I had thought that, you'd certainly have disabused me of the notion by now.'

Jules began adjusting his controls, and their craft swooped down toward the escaping limousine. 'I think I had best disabuse some people of a few other notions,' he said, never taking his eyes from the forward screen. 'Such as the notion that they can attack us and expect to get away with it.'

As the occupants of the limousine drove away from the scene of the blast, their only worry – and it was a minor one – was that they might run into some police on this return journey. But the way ahead of them looked perfectly clear of any traffic, and they did not think to look upward.

Suddenly their limo was rocked by a beam from above. With pinpoint accuracy, Jules had narrowed his car's multiblasters down to needle beams of ferocious intensity and shot off the two tires on the righthand side. The speeding limousine skidded, swerved, slewed into the embankment by the side of the road and finally overturned, rolling end over end three times before coming to rest upside down.

Jules brought his craft down in a quick swoop beside the

stricken limo, and he and Vonnie raced out of either side, stun-guns drawn. The three men they found inside the wreck were all too dazed by the crash to offer any resistance, but the d'Alemberts gave them each a number two stun anyway just to keep them out of mischief for the next few minutes. Then they tied their captives up and tossed them in the back of the SOTE craft. Jules took off again and, on a whim, turned his blasters full force on the wreckage of the limo. The ground vehicle shattered, bursting apart into a cloud of wreckage that would never be identified as the limousine it had once been. Once again, mystery would enshroud the interlopers, confusing the enemy further.

Jules placed a vidicom call to Panji, who had been waiting anxiously to hear the results of Chactan's raid. 'You placed your bet on the wrong side, Panji,' he said. 'Too bad. I wish I could say it had been nice knowing you, but it hasn't. Is your will up to date?' And he broke the connection without waiting for a reply.

'We're not really going to kill him, are we?' Vonnie asked.

'Of course not. He's too useful to us as a go-between. But he's due for some close calls he'll never forget.'

The men they had captured were just low-ranking blaster-bats, hardly goldmines of information about the arms smuggling operation. They did, however, provide the d'Alemberts with Chactan's name and the addresses of three of his warehouses. The agents then turned the captives over to the local SOTE people, as they'd done with Panji's body-guards, asking that they be kept out of circulation until this affair was over.

'Think we have enough information to let the local police take over the investigation?' Vonnie asked her husband.

Jules shook his head. 'I don't like doing an incomplete job. All we've got is a name and some places where the arms are stored. If we let the police handle it from here, they'll nail Chactan and confiscate his merchandise, but someone new will merely take over the practice. Chactan has to be getting his weapons from somewhere. All the legitimate munitions works are imperially licensed and monitored; if there were any inventory losses big enough to account for all these sales, they would have been noticed by now.'

'Which means Chactan or the people behind him have set

up an illicit armory,' Yvonne said thoughtfully. 'They're manufacturing their own weapons independently.'

'Precisely, *ma cherie*. You're catching on quickly. And *that's* what we have to find and put out of commission, not some small-time local supplier.'

From that point on, the war between Chactan's forces and Jules's 'organization' escalated to enormous proportions. But it was a very one-sided war. Chactan would find his warehouses destroyed, his guards all vanished. Rendezvous with prospective buyers would be raided by hooded figures who hijacked the cargo and disappeared into thin air. The raids against his organization became increasingly bold, and Chactan seemed powerless to prevent them. He sent out feelers through the local underworld to discover any leads toward the identity of the people behind his misfortune, but there was no information to be gained at any price. The only conclusion reached was that these people were total outsiders who had suddenly and dramatically entered the picture.

Panji, meanwhile, was suffering through a series of his own tortures. As Jules had promised, the 'close calls' were coming frequently. A bomb planted in his groundcar exploded prematurely, destroying his garage but sparing his life. A flowerpot falling from a high window ledge just barely missed him as he was walking along the street. A blaster bolt shot through his bedroom window one night as he was undressing for sleep, narrowly missing him and burning a hole deep into his wall. Panji was rapidly becoming a nervous wreck, and he was communicating his nervousness loudly to Chactan.

The munitions boss was getting pressured from another side as well. He suddenly found himself the recipient of long subcom calls from Duke Morro of Tregania wondering what was holding up the operation. 'I've got reports to make, and there's nothing to say,' the Duke complained. 'You know *he* doesn't like that.'

Both men knew to whom the pronoun referred: their mutual boss, known to them only as 'C', whose communications reached them only via telecom and who, to the best of their knowledge, had never been seen by anyone. But despite the mystery of his identity, there was no doubt about how he treated subordinates who failed to perform their assigned functions.

'*He* wants results,' the Duke reiterated in his high pitched whine. 'We can't keep up our end of the program with these interlopers cutting off our trade.'

'I can't destroy what I can't find!' Chactan snarled. The Duke's whining always made him edgy, and he was already feeling frustrated enough at being unable to handle the menace. 'But tell him things will be back to normal within a week.' And he angrily broke the connection.

Chactan, like all the others in C's organization, had certain specific goals he must achieve, but he had broad discretionary powers about how to attain them. An idea was forming in the back of his mind. It might not be necessary to fight these newcomers, after all. They just wanted money and power – they had no aims higher than that. He could give them what they wanted and still work toward his own ends if he offered them a partnership in his own operation. If *you can't beat them*, he modified the old adage, *have them join you*.

He called Panji. 'I want you to contact those people, tell them we're ready to deal.'

'I don't know where they are, any more than you do.'

'Still, you're the only one so far who's had any contact with them at all. You'll think of something.'

Panji was reluctant to have any further communication with those people, but Chactan pressured him mercilessly until he gave in. Figuring that they were still watching him, Panji put up a big sign in front of his house reading, 'Truce. Please call for important message.'

Within an hour the vidicom rang and he heard Jules's voice. 'What's the matter, Panji? Isn't it a little late for apologies?'

The arms merchant could not help but let his nervousness show through. 'My, uh, supplier would like to arrange a meeting with you.'

'Like the last time? That was a little one-sided.'

'He says you can pick the terms of the rendezvous. He just wants to talk to you about joining forces and forming an even bigger organization, with more profits for everybody.'

Jules and Yvonne, on the other end of the line, exchanged

glances and smiles. They were being invited inside, where they could see the conspiracy's inner workings for themselves. So far, Jules's plan was working perfectly.

CHAPTER SEVEN

PIAS THE PREACHER

Neither Pias nor Yvette spoke much as they drove back to their boarding house. They weren't accustomed to having their plans blow up in their faces so dramatically and, now that they were safely away from the dangerous situation, the shock was beginning to set in. They sat together in silence, each mentally reviewing the events of the evening and wondering where they had made their mistakes.

Not until they were back at their home base did they open up and talk about the disaster at the Clunard administrative complex. Pias described his encounter with the mysterious woman who moved faster than any living creature he'd ever seen and also was immune to a stun-gun charge. 'I can't have missed,' he said. 'I was at point blank range. But she kept on coming.'

Yvette paused before answering. 'This is something I've been worried about ever since we saw that exhortation, and I'd say our little *contretemps* tonight has verified my suspicions. Did I ever tell you about Jules's and my adventure during the Princess's Progress on Ansegria?'

'I don't think so.'

'There's so much you have to catch up on. I wish we'd known each other longer.'

Pias smiled wanly. 'The feeling's mutual.'

Yvette returned the smile. 'That wasn't exactly what I was thinking of, but it is a nice thought. Back to the subject. On Ansegria, Jules and I encountered a robot that had been fashioned to look exactly like a human being. It was immensely strong, incredibly fast and virtually undetectable except with special instruments. A stun-gun would have no effect on it, because it doesn't have a nervous system; you need something a little more definite, like a blaster. Vonnie actually destroyed the one on Ansegria by electrocuting it.'

Pias nodded slowly. 'So that's what we're up against.'

'It has to be. We learned a little while later that there were at least three other humanoid robots created at the same time each with its own specific mission . . .'

'I remember now your saying something about that. Jules just destroyed one a little while ago at Edna's wedding, didn't he?'

Yvette nodded. 'Yes, the one that had been fashioned to look like Lady Bloodstar. Which leaves at least two to go. We know a couple of additional facts – one is male and the other female . . . and *both* of the ones we know about were constructed to look like natives of heavy gravity worlds like DesPlaines or Purity.'

'Or Newforest,' Pias said quietly.

Yvette's eyes widened. 'Your brother!'

Pias Bavol was the eldest child of the Duke of Newforest. As such, he had the title of marquis and the right to inherit the planet after his father's death. But his younger brother Tas, through chicanery, had gotten him banished from Newforest on charges that he was deserting his people – and Pias, because his work for SOTE was top secret, could not defend himself from those charges. His dying father had disowned him, cutting him off from all inheritance as though he had never existed. Though Pias normally affected a cheerful mien, Yvette knew that the wounds from his banishment went quite deep.

'I really don't know,' Pias replied softly. 'The real Tas was certainly nasty enough to do all that without any outside interference. I don't want to point the finger of suspicion without stronger evidence to go on, or it would merely look like sour grapes. We can't be positive Tas is the male robot – but we sure as hell know where the female is, don't we?'

Yvette nodded. The subject of his brother and his birthright was obviously not one that Pias wanted to discuss right now, so she was just as willing to change the topic. 'That explains how Tresa Clunard was able to bend that metal bar – she's a robot passing off her superhuman strength as "miracles". And it means something else, too.' Her expression darkened. 'It confirms the Head's worst suspicions about the uses to which this Army of the Just will be put. The robots seem to be a major weapon in Lady A's arsenal, and she doesn't deploy them arbitrarily. She must have some future plans for this private army, important ones. We'll have to notify the Head of this development immediately.'

'Does that mean SOTE will step in officially to crush this threat?'

'I don't think so. You have to remember there are something like twenty or thirty planets within the Empire that were founded exclusively as religious retreats – Purity, Delf, Anares, Shambalah, Arborea and so on. If the Emperor acts officially in a manner that looks like he's quashing religious freedom – even though the motivations are entirely different – the repercussions could be enormous. Lady A and her gang were quite clever to cloak this force under the guise of religious zealots. Even if we had incontrovertible evidence that this was a nonsectarian plot to overthrow the Emperor, I know the Head well enough to know he would prefer surreptitious action. It's still up to us to break up this army from the inside, so they could never accuse the Empire of interfering.'

'That might not be too difficult. The entire structure is built around the charisma of Tresa Clunard. Without her, there would be nothing. She preaches against sin, against evil, against *machines* – there's the ultimate irony, she's a machine herself. If we can expose her as one, her followers would be so disenchanted that the army would break up of its own accord.'

'Getting the proof to satisfy them won't be easy. They're true believers, remember; that sort is hard to sway from an opinion once they get it into their heads. We'd practically have to break the robot apart and pull out all the gears before they'd believe us.'

'Then that's what we'll do.' Pias had a grim smile on his face. The robot had scared him so badly tonight that the thought of pulling it to pieces in front of its admirers was positively enthralling.

They got a little rest, and then the next morning Yvette composed a coded note to the Head, explaining their theories. She and Pias did not have a subcom unit with them for direct personal communication – but a letter addressed personally to the Head with a Class Six priority and the code signature Periwinkle, delivered to the local SOTE office, would ensure the note's reaching its destination within, at most, three days' time. As an afterthought, she added her own suspicions that Tas Bavol might be one of Lady A's robots, and requested that the Head order the Newforest office of SOTE to make some discreet checks to determine whether or not that was so. After all, Pias might want to forget the matter, but Yvette could not forget. The man she loved had been deeply hurt, and Yvette made a solemn vow that sooner or later Tas Bavol would pay for that.

Their plans for exposing Tresa Clunard as a robot were more easily made then executed. To have the proper effect, the exposure had to be made publicly; and yet, such was the counselor's popularity that Pias and Yvette knew it must be done carefully, or they would be torn apart by an angry mob before they had a chance to explain.

They became regular attendees of Clunard's exhortations, following the counselor around to the various cities and villages all over Purity. But their abortive raid on her headquarters had tipped their hand; the opposition now knew that they were out there somewhere, and had started taking elaborate security precautions. Whenever Tresa Clunard appeared in public, she was surrounded by a squadron of guards. The guards were inconspicuous unless one knew what to look for, but Pias and Yvette could spot them a kilometer away. In private, the cordon around her was even tighter. Security had been beefed up, too, throughout her administrative offices.

After more than a week of frustration, Pias was ready to give up this line of offense. 'It's not impossible to destroy her,' he sighed. 'But unless it's done absolutely right, it won't have the effect we want – probably just the opposite effect, as a matter of fact. She'd come out looking like some kind of martyr. I think a change of strategy is called for.'

'Oh?' Yvette raised an eyebrow. 'And have you finally devised this vaunted plan you keep promising?'

'As a matter of fact,' her husband replied, 'I have. It's a way to achieve our own ends and, at the same time, bring a little cheer to the lives of these poor benighted Puritans.'

'They don't want cheer, they want salvation.'

'They want both, if only they knew it – and I can give it to them. What's the primary form of entertainment on Purity?'

'There isn't any,' Yvette said. 'They don't allow sensables, trivision, radio, theater, sporting events, music – they're all too decadent, and take one's mind off the serious business of achieving salvation. Even the Circus has never been allowed here, and we're the most innocent entertainment in the Empire.'

'You're right that they ban a lot of things, but you're dead wrong if you think they don't have entertainment. What do you think Tresa Clunard provides? How about all the other minor league "exhorters" who swarm around the countryside like locusts? Haven't you felt the emotional intensity at Clunard's shows?'

'Now that you mention it – yes, there is a great element of theatricality to what she does.'

'Of course there is. All people need some cathartic outlet for pent up feelings or they'll go mad. The more restrictive a society, the stronger that need is. The only socially acceptable way of expressing anything on Purity is through religion, so that's the form their catharsis takes. People come in droves to attend a show and have some well-spoken showman tell them how sinful they've been lately. They eat it up.'

'I haven't noticed you being pure enough to set a good example,' Yvette kidded. 'You'd have a hard time fitting into the mold they want.'

'All it takes is wit, charm and good looks – all of which you must admit I possess in overabundance.'

'You left out modesty.'

'When you have all the talents I have, you don't *need* modesty. But seriously, I don't intend to fit into their common mold, because I don't want to just blend in. I want to come in with a message directly counter to what Clunard is pushing – that people can still be holy while accepting modern conveniences. As long as I keep mentioning God and sin, I'll be socially acceptable – but if I can make any serious dent in Clunard's audiences, she'll consider us a threat, and come after us. That may give us the opportunity to make our move.'

74

Yvette nodded slowly. She knew from her fighting training that when an opponent reached out to strike a blow, he usually left an opening that the clever fighter could utilize – if the blow could be blocked first. 'It might work,' she admitted. 'But first you have to become such a whirlwind preacher that you represent some danger to her movement.'

'Just watch. I am going to become the most astonishing preacher this sorry old planet has ever seen.'

He set about his plan by breaking most of the rules Purity's counselors lived by. Spurning the traditional brown or gray robes, he had local tailors shaking their heads in bewilderment at the outfit he requested. The shirt and trousers were of nal's wool, and were pure dazzling white – as were the knee-high suede boots for his feet. His belt would be of thin hammered silver, and over this ensemble, open down the front, would be a shiny white caftan with a train trailing a meter and a half behind him. When he was on the stage, he wanted to leave his audience starstruck.

Traditionally, counselors did little to advertise their exhortations; a small box in the local newsroll listing the name of the speaker, the time and the place was considered adequate, plus a sign outside the meeting hall for several days before the event. Pias, however, saw no reason to hide himself behind a curtain of hypocritical modesty, so he insisted on running full page ads in the newsrolls for a week before he made an appearance; he had handbills printed up and postered on every available wall. He had flyers mailed to every home in the district where he would be speaking. If there had been radio or trivision available he would have advertised there as well. He toyed with the idea of staging parades, but Yvette – thinking that would be much too outré for Puritan audiences – talked him out of it.

He started his tour in the smaller towns, planning to build a reputation there that would carry him into the cities on a wave of popularity. The rural communities were also an easier target, because so little ever happened there that anything out of the ordinary was bound to stir up a great deal of attention.

The townsfolk did not know what to make of Cromwell Hanrahan, the previously unheralded preacher with the cocky manner and the bold new presentation. There were many who considered him shocking, saying that a counselor, above all his fellows, should be modest and humble in God's sight; if *he* didn't set the example of the pure, simple life, then who would? There were others who, though they would never have admitted it aloud, were secretly titillated that someone had come along and dared be as open and flashy as they wished they could be. There were even some people who fit into both categories at once. But whatever their thoughts were about this strange new counselor, the fact was that they flocked to his exhortations in record numbers.

Pias did not disappoint them. He strode out onto the stage with a brash confidence that reminded Yvette of her several-times-removed cousin Henri d'Alembert, the Circus's chief barker. Pias's voice boomed out across the hall as he spoke, and he used his hands to dramatic effect with gesticulations that emphasized his meaning.

'Brothers and sisters,' he began, 'we all love God. I can see by your faces as I look out over this audience that you're all good people, concerned with the salvation of your souls. But you've become so proud of your own righteousness that you're turning your backs on God's handiwork, throwing away the gifts that God intended you to have. I tell you, brothers and sisters, the Lord looks with disfavor on a man who spurns what his God has freely offered.'

At this point, Pias could tell that his audience was stunned into silence. They were used to counselors exhorting them to give more of themselves to God; no one ever spoke of God giving anything to them. Their curiosity would only make them more receptive.

'How often do we hear of the blessedness of giving? How often are we reminded that we must give to others to make ourselves more worthy of divine grace? The holy books of every religion tell us the same thing: that to give freely and openly of our own riches to those less fortunate than ourselves is to practice the highest form of nobility. The blessed St Paul himself ranked charity above even hope and faith. Is that not true?'

There was a slight murmur through the crowd now. They could scarcely deny that point, but they still did not see where Pias's speech would lead them.

'Surely if that is true, then it must be a sin to deny a person the chance to exercise his charity. If someone better off than yourself offers you a gift of his own free will, then to repel his offer is to deny him the divine grace his action would otherwise have earned him. You are taking his salvation upon yourself by refusing to allow him to obtain God's favor. Brothers and sisters, I submit that God alone has the right and the power to judge such matters.

'Surely, then, what we have been doing is a millionfold worse. God has laden this Universe with riches beyond our understanding, given it to us to use for His greater glory. The wonders of it are beyond numbering, its bounties are beyond comprehension. Yet here we sit, living our "pure and simple life", denying the gifts that God has freely given us. We are so wrapped up in our own righteousness that we are marching ourselves straight into Hell.

'God gave us our eyes, so that we might see the beauty of nature. He has created all about us. God gave us our ears, so that we might hear the sweet harmony of all His creatures. He gave us our mouths and noses so that we might enjoy the delicious tastes and heavenly aromas He has set like a banquet before us. These are gifts beyond price that He has given to us freely, because of His love for us. Praise the Lord for His bounteous gifts.'

There were a few straggling echoes of 'Praise the Lord', throughout the audience, but most of the people remained in silence as they did during Clunard's exhortations. Perhaps it was expected of them, or perhaps they were wondering whether this new preacher was a madman or a heretic. The things he was saying made sense, yet felt as though they were starting to contradict what Puritans had been taught all their lives.

Pias was not going to let them get away with so pitiful a response. 'I said, praise the Lord for His bounteous gifts.'

This time the crowd reaction was a little more favorable, but still not up to the standard Pias wanted to set. He had to show the crowd that he controlled it, that it must do what he commanded. 'For the sake of your souls, sinners,' he yelled at them, 'shout it out. Make the walls shake and the ceiling shudder with the sound of your love for God. Praise the Lord!'

This time he got what he wanted. The answering response was not quite enough to rattle the rafters, but it was a good, healthy shout. It would get stronger over the course of the evening, now that the pattern had been set.

Pias was just warming up to his topic, and he could feel the fire of his performance flowing through himself. He strode back and forth across the stage like a caged panther, swinging the train of his caftan in majestic arcs, staring down the doubts of the audience, defying anyone to deny the truth of his claims.

'But you have turned your backs on God,' he bellowed. Swirling the caftan's train around his right forearm, he pointed an accusing finger and swept the arm to encompass his entire audience. 'You have said, "To deny my eyes a look at His beauty is holy." You have said, "To deny my ears the pleasure of His music is blessed." You have said, "To deny my senses the tastes and smells that God intended for them is the highest form of worship." In doing so, you reject all the gifts God has laid before us. You reject God Himself, for is not God *in* all the wonders that He has created? Oh you sinners, fear for your souls, for you have denied the gifts of God!'

One woman cried out in anguish, and Pias knew he had the audience where he wanted it. He was getting into more familiar territory now as far as they were concerned, and they could accept more of what he said. There is nothing a Puritan loves quite so much as to be berated for how sinful he is. He regards such a purging of his soul like a more hedonistic man might view a soothing bath; it allows him to emerge afterward feeling cleaner, more refreshed.

Pias continued to pound his theme home. 'God gave us our hands, the most marvelous tools in the Universe. He gave them to us that we might use them to build, to create as He created, so that we might truly be in His image. He intended us to make order out of chaos, to the greater glory of His name.

'But what do you do with these divine hands that He gave you? You hoard them and their talents, like the wicked and slothful servant of the parable. You till the land for survival, fashion the simplest tools and the plainest buildings, and think that thereby you are fulfilling your obligation to God.

Instead, you false thinkers, you are cheating God of the glory that is His due. I say woe unto you, and fear the imminent wrath of God! For, as with that unprofitable servant of the parable, you will be cast into outer darkness, and there shall be weeping and gnashing of teeth!'

There were wails of woe from the audience, and Pias paused to let them run their course before he continued. 'God's greatest gift of all is our minds. He gave us these magnificent instruments to explore the puzzles He has put before us, and each new secret we discover about the Universe only makes us appreciate the miracles of God still further. But you, you righteous sinners, you turn away from the miracles of science, the miracles which God gave Man the ability to find. There are those who say that technology is evil, that because it eases the burden of our existence it must therefore be wrong. But I say that technology is a blessing that God has given us, that we may marvel even more at the wonders He has created. Did He not give us the brains with which to create machines? Are we to spurn His gift of intellect, to live our lives in misery and ignorance like the animals above which we were obviously set? I say that to do so is to insult God, to reject His gifts, to cast aside His love. I say that to continue as we are is the worst sin imaginable, and we all deserve our damnation for eternity in the fiery, everburning pits of Hell.'

Pias had taken everything the Puritans believed and twisted it around a hundred and eighty degrees. He had preached epicureanism to stoics, hedonism to ascetics, broken every code they knew. And yet so expertly had he played the game, so skillfully had he manipulated their emotions, that they ended up loving it. By the time he had finished, nearly a quarter of the audience was dedicated to his cause, and more than half the rest were at least tolerant of his ideas.

'Well,' he asked Yvette after his first performance, 'what do you think now?'

'I think,' she said, 'that if you can keep on consistently like this, it will make Tresa Clunard and her Army of the Just sit up and take notice.'

And she was right.

CHAPTER EIGHT

SLAG

The meeting with Chactan the arms supplier would be a big one, and naturally Jules and Yvonne chose to dress up for the occasion. Jules sported a mustache and wore contact lenses that changed his eye color from gray to brown. He darkened his complexion, added a few creases to his face and insinuated the faintest bit of gray into his hair, all of which gave him the appearance of being a decade older than he really was.

Vonnie dyed her normally brown hair red and plucked out her eyebrows until they were just the thinnest of lines separating her eyelids from her forehead. She covered her face and hands, and all other exposed areas of skin, with the glittering body makeup that was the rage of Sector Thirty-One, and wore boots with heels that added a full six centimeters to her height.

The meeting was to take place in the center of an open field, where there was a clear view for kilometers around. That would prevent Chactan and his cohorts from planning any kind of ambush. The d'Alemberts arrived in their groundcar two hours early to check out the landscape and, when they had assured themselves there were no tricks, they sat in the craft and waited for the others to arrive.

Five minutes before the appointed hour, Chactan's copter came into view over the horizon. It flew at a leisurely pace and settled to earth twenty meters from the d'Alembert car. As Jules had instructed, Chactan and Panji were the only two people inside. They stepped out of the copter, arms extended to either side to show they were carrying no weapons. Jules nodded to his wife, and the two SOTE agents climbed out of their own vehicle. The four people met at a spot midway between the two crafts.

Chactan was not a physically impressive man. He was of medium height and build, with a dark complexion and weathered hands. He was partially bald and possessed of craggy good looks. But his walk and his mannerisms revealed him to be a man brimming with self-confidence, not to be crossed lightly. So far, the d'Alemberts' dealings with Panji had been simple, but this Chactan would be no easy opponent.

'Khorosho, we're here,' Jules said as he and Vonnie approached the other pair. 'We've been delegated to speak for our organization. What have you got to say?'

It was Chactan who replied; Panji had been brought along merely to provide someone familiar to these unknown interlopers, and would take no real part in the negotiations. 'This struggle between us has to stop. It's taking too heavy a toll on both sides.'

'Really! I hadn't noticed any toll on our side.'

If Jules's remark had any effect on Chactan, he masked it nicely. 'There haven't been any profits, though, either. Blowing up our shipments hasn't automatically brought you business. The customers you've tried to steal from us haven't been able to get any merchandise, from what we hear on the street. You've been spending so much of your energy hitting us that you haven't had time to do any selling of your own. And that's what business is really about, isn't it?'

Jules stood silently for a moment, then gave a slow nod. 'Even if what you say is true, we still hold the upper hand. The market is still there, unfulfilled. If we continue on as we are, we'll starve you out and then have it all to ourselves.'

'Do you think so?' Chactan raised an eyebrow inquisitively. 'If we leave our customers unsatisfied too much longer, someone else will move in to supply their needs. Then you'll have to get rid of him, too. You'll be spending all your time and money just to get rid of competition, and you won't have any chance to make a profit. I don't think you can continue operating that way much longer.'

'I presume you're here to offer an alternative.'

'Yes, a partnership. We're not greedy – rather than continuing to lose so much of our investment to your inroads, we'd take you in and let you work with us, sharing the profits accordingly.'

'What can you do for us that we can't do for ourselves?' Yvonne spoke up for the first time.

Chactan turned to face her. 'We've got the contacts ready made; it could take you months, or even years, to develop a network the size of ours. We've already got the customers, and a distribution set up to serve their needs.'

'We've got a few customers too, that you probably don't know anything about.' Vonnie dropped that little comment and watched Chactan's eyes light up. If he was plugged into Lady A's conspiracy, that piece of news would travel quickly back to headquarters. 'We get our merchandise from a couple of small manufacturers who operate double inventory systems to fool the impers. What about you?'

Chactan smiled, glad of the opportunity to show off the superiority of his own organization. 'We don't have to bother with complications like that. We have our own plant hidden away, providing top notch goods exclusively for us.'

They had already guessed that, but Jules and Yvonne pretended to be excited by this revelation. They asked for a moment alone and pretended to confer among themselves. Then they asked Chactan for the plant's location, but he wouldn't tell them. They asked technical questions about the plant's operating capacity and output, number of employees and profit margins. Chactan answered some questions specifically while leaving others vague or totally ignored.

Jules and Vonnie next asked for some time alone in their car while they talked to 'other executives' in their organization. They put on a good show of arguing over the radio in their car, out of earshot of Chactan and Panji, helping to convince those two that the SOTE agents were part of a larger group and not merely on their own. Finally they emerged from their car once more and approached the central meeting spot.

'We agree,' Jules said, 'on one condition. We have to inspect your plant to make sure it's producing up to our standards.'

Chactan shook his head. 'But if you don't like it, that still gives you the opportunity to back out, knowing where our plant is and able to cause still more damage to us, without risking a thing yourselves.'

'What do you suggest, then?' Vonnie asked.

'You give us the list of these other customers you mentioned. It'll be an equal deal, a secret for a secret. If we're going to end up partners, we would end up sharing the information anyway.'

Jules and Yvonne glanced at one another, and then Vonnie nodded. '*Khorosho*, you've got a deal.'

There was, of course, no list of customers that the d'Alemberts' organization had been supplying. Jules and Yvonne spent a full day making up a convincing-sounding list of names. For the sake of thoroughness, they transmitted a copy of the list to the local SOTE office, with instructions that these names were to be entered in the Service's official files in case Chactan's people ran a detailed check.

Another snag occurred when Chactan balked at letting the d'Alemberts take their own ship to the secret world where the munitions plant was hidden. His reasoning was logical: the d'Alemberts had already proven their hostile intentions toward his organization, and if he simply told them where the plant was they could fly over it and bomb it to smithereens. Jules and Vonnie countered that if they went in one of Chactan's ships, some 'accident' might befall them.

A compromise was finally developed. Two ships would make the journey, *La Comète Cuivré* and one of Chactan's. Chactan would accompany Jules in the *Comet*, while Vonnie would travel with the crew from the other side; each would serve as hostage to the other's good behavior. The d'Alemberts were a little reluctant to allow Chactan aboard their vessel because of all the top secret equipment it contained, but they realized there was no other logical way of achieving their goal. They hid as much of the special SOTE equipment as they could, and disguised the rest to look like ordinary spaceship gear. They were fortunate in that George Chactan was not himself a licensed pilot, and had little idea what was supposed to be there and what wasn't.

Once they had blasted off the surface of Nampur, Chactan gave Jules the directions to head for the system containing the planet Tregania, twenty-three lightyears away. Jules handed Chactan the envelope containing the names of his fictitious customers, and they were on their way.

Once they reached the new solar system, Chactan ordered Jules to go, not to Tregania, which was the fourth planet out from the sun, but to the first planet, which had no official name. There, safe from prying eyes, the munitions plant was in full operation. The people who worked on that world had given it the singularly appropriate nickname of Slag.

Slag was an airless ball of rock ten thousand kilometers in diameter, orbiting a mere fifty-three million kilometers from its sun. As far as anyone outside the conspiracy knew, it was both uninhabited and uninhabitable. Temperatures on the daytime hemisphere were in excess of three hundred and fifty celsius, hot enough that pools of molten lead and rivers of flowing tin were conceivable, if not commonplace. On the night side, the temperatures plummeted to just slightly above absolute zero. Nobody gave Slag much of a thought when there were so many more planets perfectly suitable for human habitation. That was what made it such a perfect hiding place.

As the *Comet* approached this barren world, a signal was beamed out to the ship, giving landing instructions so that it could set down near the base. As Jules came in low, he saw that landing was a feat that would tax to the limit his abilities as a pilot. The ground was so cracked from the alternating periods of searing heat and bitter cold that it was difficult to find a smooth, open area in which to set his ship down. Other ships were clustered about on a small plain, including the ship that Vonnie had traveled aboard. After receiving radioed assurances that everything was smooth with her, Jules completed the ticklish task of bringing the *Comet* down within the tiny zone provided.

A passenger tube snaked out from the main dome of the factory, attaching itself to the *Comet*'s hatch and forming an airtight seal. Jules and Chactan walked down the tube to the base without ever having to don their spacesuits.

Despite the fact that this was a large factory for the manufacture of munitions, the base had a temporary look to it. Indeed, the dome *did* have to be periodically taken apart and relocated elsewhere on the planet, because Slag rotated on its axis once every fifty-four days while it revolved around the sun in seventy-seven days. It did not keep one face perpetually toward its primary, as Luna did to Earth.

The base, being this close to the sun, used solar power to run its generators rather than nuclear power which was common through the rest of the Galaxy, and had to stay on the sunny side to remain in operation.

Jules was reunited with Yvonne in the main reception lock, a large chamber with windows looking out onto the landing field. The two were then taken off to the living quarters so they could be settled in. They had not told Chactan that they were married – they wanted to keep him guessing about their identities and relationship – so he had conservatively assigned them to separate rooms. Neither Jules nor Yvonne was excited by the idea of sleeping apart so recently after their marriage, but they were resigned to it as simply one more sacrifice to be made in the service of their Emperor. Vonnie did manage to whisper in Jules's ear how much she would miss him, and Jules squeezed her hand to show he reciprocated.

As they walked back with Chactan toward the Mess Hall, Jules asked, 'I can see that this is a great hiding place for your factory, but is there any other reason for its being here? The operational costs must be far higher than they would be on a more habitable planet.'

'True. But we get our raw materials for nothing.' Chactan waved a hand expansively. 'This entire world is one vast chemical laboratory. Metals that you normally have to dig out of the ground, smelt down, and refine are flowing freely in their molten state, relatively pure. Of those materials that remain solid, we have unlimited solar energy available to help us break them down into more usable form. Energy, resources and secrecy are the three big advantages to Slag. The inconvenience of maintaining the base is at most a minor disadvantage by comparison.'

In the crowded situation that existed on Slag, the Mess Hall doubled as a recreation room, and there were several hundred people scattered about at the various tables, playing electronic games, gambling at cards or merely whiling away the time with talk. 'How many people are stationed here?' Jules asked as the party made its way to the food dispenser.

'About two thousand,' Chactan replied. 'The exact number depends on how busy we are at any given time.' He ordered his food from the dispenser, then moved to a vacant spot at one of the long tables. After a moment, Jules and Vonnie joined him.

'Large portions of the plant are automated,' the criminal leader continued as they ate. 'We obviously don't want to have any more people involved in the operation than is absolutely necessary, both from a standpoint of safety and from a standpoint of secrecy. We do need some people, though, to run the machines, to help take them down, move them and set them up again whenever night starts overtaking us, to scout the geological locations for usable resources, and to mine the resources once we find them.'

'It sounds fascinating,' Yvonne said, genuinely interested. She had never visited so hostile a world before, and found the concept of living and working here most exciting.

'The entire operation is extremely efficient,' Chactan beamed with justifiable pride. It was clear he had established this base himself, and it was his expertise that made it work. The admiration Yvonne was showing made him open up more than he normally might have.

After their meal they toured the production facilities and watched munitions being manufactured through all stages of their development. They saw chemicals mixed in large vats to create the plastics that were poured into molds and shaped into the gun bodies. They saw metals being smelted down and formed into the interior components of blasters and casings for bombs. They visited the mixing rooms in a separate complex, where highly volatile compounds were combined to form powerful explosives. The plant even manufactured its own fuses.

'We specialize in the acid-mix type,' Chactan explained. 'Acids of all sorts are very plentiful around here.'

Jules and Yvonne nodded knowingly. Acid-mix fuses were among the simplest kinds to use. A small vial of acid was broken in the top container of the fuse. The center of the container was made of a material that the acid would eat away, until eventually it reached the second half of the container. There it mixed with another compound, generating enough heat to detonate the bomb to which it was attached. The length of time it took to detonate could be altered by varying the strength of the acid and the thickness of the material it had to eat through. It was all totally automatic, and could be explained to anyone with normal intelligence, so it was the natural device to give to terrorists with little technical training.

As they made their way back to the living quarters, Vonnie remarked, 'I'm very impressed with what I've seen, but there's one omission. You've got all strengths of blasters, bombs, explosives and fuses, but I haven't seen any stun-guns being manufactured here.'

'We don't make them,' Chactan said flatly. 'Stunners are not a fearsome enough weapon, and our customers don't want them. In order to spread terror, they have to plant in people the certain knowledge that they will die if they disobey orders. Nothing does that better than a bomb or a blaster.'

He gave a snort. 'Stunners are gentlemen's weapons, a promise not to hurt the victim permanently if he plays by the rules. We don't follow those rules. We play for keeps.'

'I'll keep that in mind,' Jules said solemnly.

During the 'night' shift, while Jules and Vonnie were asleep, a message came over the telecom machine installed in the base's communications and control office. The woman on duty requested a printout, then delivered it personally to Chactan's room.

After the woman had left, Chactan unfolded the note and read it privately, becoming more and more disturbed at its consequences. He had sent the list of customers Jules had provided to his boss, C, for further checking. The reply did not please him:

CUSTOMERS DID NOT EXIST IN SOTE'S FILES UNTIL DAY BEFORE YOUR QUERY. DO NOT EXIST ANYWHERE ELSE. SUSPECT SOTE AGENT ACTIVITY.

As was the standard procedure with all communications from his boss, he burned it immediately after reading it, then summoned Ray Furman, the plant manager, to his room. While he waited for the man to arrive, he coldly considered his alternatives.

'I made a serious mistake,' he admitted when Furman showed up, 'but fortunately it's not an incorrectable one. The two people I brought with me today have turned out to be SOTE agents. Naturally, we can't let them leave Slag alive.'

Furman nodded. 'I understand. They're sleeping right now. I could round up a couple of men and ...'

'It's too risky to do anything inside the base,' Chactan said, shaking his head. 'They're armed right now, and they might end up doing some damage to the plant before we kill them. I don't want anything to endanger our operation here.'

'What do you suggest, then?'

Chactan smiled. 'They were scheduled to go out tomorrow with one of the mining teams to see how that phase of our process works. We'll just let them go. After all, Slag is a very inhospitable world – all sorts of accidents can happen, can't they?'

CHAPTER NINE

PANIC IN THE HALL

On Purity, in the main offices of Tresa Clunard, there was little cause for happiness. Elspeth FitzHugh, the counselor's chief assistant, was presenting the weekly figures for recruitment into their Army of the Just. 'As you can see, Sister Tresa,' FitzHugh said, 'the figures show a decline for the third straight week.'

Clunard took the papers from her aide's hand and skimmed the columns of numbers quickly. The drop in recruits was all too obvious. What was worse, the figures were dropping off by larger amounts every week. If this trend were to continue unabated, within two weeks there would be virtually no new recruits joining her army.

She looked up from her chair at the woman standing before her. 'Would you care to venture any opinions about why this is happening, Sister Elspeth?' she asked. 'Is it because they're getting tired of listening to me? Am I asking the impossible of them?'

'You're asking no more than you're willing to give yourself,' FitzHugh soothed. 'And as for getting tired of listening, I'd have to say that the crowds seem to be as enthusiastic as they ever were.'

'Yes, but they're smaller. Even I can see that, despite the lights shining in my eyes.'

FitzHugh could not deny such an unquestionable fact. Instead, she nudged the subject in a slightly new direction. 'I think it's because of this new counselor, this Cromwell Hanrahan. His dress and his manner of speech are outrageous and his exhortations refute every principle you stand for. He uses the twisted logic of Satan himself to make sin sound holy, and tells people that their wicked thoughts and deeds are ordained by God. He preys upon the weakness in people's minds, whereas you try to build up the strengths. The sinners want to believe him because he offers them the easy path. He offers them pleasure; you only offer them hard work and devotion to God.'

Clunard nodded. 'That's true. God must have placed him in my path as a further test of my faith. I'll have to work even harder to prove myself and my cause.'

'I think you should do more than that.'

Clunard stopped and looked at her. 'What do you mean?'

'I mean that Hanrahan is our enemy. You are right, God sent him to us as a test of your faith and your will. You have spoken out well against sinners like Hanrahan. Perhaps it's time to be more specific.'

'You mean mention him by name, single him out as a symptom of the evil that's infected the Galaxy as a whole?'

FitzHugh shrugged. 'If that's what's necessary to rid us of the plague, then I say yes.'

'You don't fight evil by shouting at it, Sister Elspeth. I've told you that many times before. All I would be doing is advertising his heresies even further, spreading them in places he himself cannot reach.'

'Yet you must do something.'

Clunard stood up and walked to the far end of the room. She had her back turned to FitzHugh and, for a long moment, was lost in deep thought. Finally she straightened her shoulders and turned once more to look at her aide. About her face was the divine glow FitzHugh had seen there during some of the counselor's better performances.

'You're absolutely right,' Clunard said. 'I must do something. So far, all my promises to God have been accomplished through words, not deeds. It is very easy to speak out against evil, far more difficult to raise a hand against it. I have counseled, I have preached, I have strutted, amassing a force in God's name and pretending that such was my ultimate mission. But God knows the truth, and He has sent Hanrahan as a reminder to me. All our forces will be of no use to the Lord if we never use them.'

'Sending our army out against one man is a little extravagant, don't you think?'

'It needn't be the entire army,' Clunard said. 'But I can see now that Hanrahan is an evil placed in our path by God to test our resolution and our will. We shall not fail Him. Hanrahan must be exised from our midst at any cost. I

leave it to your discretion, Sister Elspeth, but I want Cromwell Hanrahan removed so that our cause of righteousness
may continue to grow.'

'As you wish, Sister Tresa,' said FitzHugh — as ever, the
model of the ideal assistant.

The signs that Tresa Clunard's crusade was in trouble
were apparent even to Pias and Yvette. After Pias had been
on the stump for three weeks preaching his gospel of religious hedonism, Yvette left him and attended a couple of
Clunard's meetings.

'There's no question about it,' she reported back to her
husband. 'Clunard's crowds are down. I think your message
is beginning to sink in.'

'Give the people what they want and they'll always come
back for more,' Pias grinned.

'But this means we have to be even more careful now.
They're not going to take this threat lying down.'

'I certainly hope not, or I'll have gone to a lot of trouble
for nothing.'

Pias was a deliberately exposed target. His gaudy figure,
sparkling white on the well-lit stage night after night, presented an easy form for any potential assassin in the audience. With the bright lights shining directly into his eyes, he
could scarcely even see beyond the first few rows of people;
there could be an army complete with cannons in the back
rows and he would never see them.

That was Yvette's responsibility. While Pias was busy
being the visible half of the team, she was practicing hard to
be invisible. She would station herself toward the back of the
audience, usually standing against the rear wall, and scan
the darkened hall for any sign of trouble. Paying no attention to her husband's words or actions, she kept her eyes
roving through the crowd for restlessness or animosity.
Most of the time the people were just confused, sometimes
offended, eventually overwhelmed. But as the weeks wore
on and their response became larger and more enthusiastic,
she knew that eventually the opposition forces would make
their move.

The first attempt came as they were returning from lunch to the hotel in the small town through which they were touring. As Pias ran the lightkey over the photosensitive lock and started to turn the knob, Yvette's sharp ears detected a slight click that should not have been there. Grabbing her husband's shirt, she yanked him hard back toward her. The two of them stumbled and fell to the ground, but fortunately each was trained enough in the art of falling that the tumble under three-gee conditions did not break any bones.

At almost the same instant, the door exploded in a burst of flames and energy that rocked the entire hotel. Fragments of the door and of the wall around it flew across the corridor and blasted large chunks out of the opposite wall. Plaster rained down from the ceiling onto the floor up and down the hallway, and windows shattered all along that side of the building.

Shaking his head to clear the ringing from his eardrums, Pias pulled himself slowly to his feet. 'You're a lifesaver, Evie,' he said, helping Yvette get up as well. 'Under the circumstances, I'll forgive your ripping my shirt.'

The inside of their room was a mess, with pieces of furniture strewn about, intermingled with burned clothing and shattered luggage. From the way the debris lay through the room, it was impossible to tell whether the people who had set the bomb had also searched the possessions for any clue to the Bavols' identities. A crowd naturally gathered, and the hotel manager came to examine the damage. Police, too, arrived to enhance the confusion, and it was more than two hours before Pias and Yvette had a chance to make a search in private. Fortunately, they had hidden all their specialized equipment quite well behind pieces of furniture, and it all survived the blast undamaged. As near as they could tell, their covers had not been exposed.

Pias gave his exhortation at the town hall that night as planned, though he was forced to wear the clothes he'd had on that afternoon because his flashier outfits had been destroyed in the explosion. This was a small town, and everyone had heard what had happened that afternoon; as a consequence, the audience was the largest of Pias's young ministerial career. If they were expecting any unusual controversy, though, they were disappointed; Pias kept strictly to his standard spiel, making no references at all to possible enemies or to threats against his life. To look at him, one would think he had spent the day relaxing in bed rather than narrowly escaping death.

Yvette, however, was a nervous wreck. She did not relax the entire evening as she kept a careful watch on the audience. Still, there were no signs of danger there, and at the end of Pias's talk the crowd gave him a most unusual round of applause for his bravery. After the exhortation, the SOTE team checked into a different hotel under other assumed names. They tried to sleep in shifts, in case assassins should strike in the middle of the night, but it ended up that neither of them got much sleep at all.

The next day was spent traveling to a new town via Purity's primitive railroad system. News of this amazing young counselor and the hint of danger about him brought a sizeable crowd out to greet him at the depot. Pias thanked them all and gave an impromptu speech, though his real talk wasn't scheduled until the next night. He did make passing reference to 'those who want to silence the Truth', and pointed out that the strategy was backfiring. He left them wanting more, which is the primary rule for any showman.

When he and Yvette reached their hotel, a new white outfit was waiting for them. Pias had wired ahead and told the tailors what he needed. A large bonus, even on Purity, assured prompt service.

The next afternoon as Pias and Yvette were emerging from a restaurant after lunch, they heard the gentle whine of a groundcar's engine accelerating. Groundcars were rare enough on Purity that the sound instantly alerted them that something out of the ordinary was about to occur. Both looked up in time to see a small car gunning down the narrow street toward them. Instinctively they split up, diving in opposite directions as low to the ground as they could get. A blaster beam sizzled the air just centimeters above them, burning its way through the stone wall of the restaurant beyond and cutting through the glass of the window.

Yvette rolled lightly to her feet. She had her own blaster

in hand, ready to fire, but thought better of it. The car had already gotten two dozen meters down the street, and was speeding away at an increasing rate. Her marksmanship was unquestionably good enough to hit the car at that distance, but she had to give some thought to the consequences. There would be a great many questions asked if the wife of a counselor were proved to have such a deadly aim with a blaster, and they would be attracting undue attention on themselves. Plus, it would alert Clunard's forces that Cromwell and Vera Hanrahan might be a little more than what they seemed.

With a slight sigh of regret, Yvette tucked her blaster back inconspicuously into the pocket of her skirt, and turned to survey the damage behind her. Pias, too, was getting to his feet, and she could see that his weapon was also half-drawn. Fortunately, no one in the immediate area had seen exactly what happened; all eyes were on the car as it sped away.

No one had been injured in the restaurant, though the damage from the blaster bolt had been extensive. Pias promised to make restitution out of the collections from his exhortations, thereby ingratiating himself further with the locals.

'It'll be soon,' Yvette remarked when the two were once more alone. 'They've tried twice and missed; they can't afford to continue that way.'

'A most comforting thought.'

'We're making them look incompetent – and what's worse, we're getting more attention and drawing larger crowds because of it. We've got public support swinging in our direction. They've got to make the definitive attempt to stop us soon.'

She tapped her fingers lightly on the top of the table in their hotel room. 'Maybe tonight.'

Both agents were well armed when they left for Pias's exhortation. Pias, as usual, carried a ministunner tucked into the sleeve of his shirt; in addition, tonight he had a small blaster tucked into the top of one boot in case the fighting became too serious. Yvette carried both stunner and blaster as well, both standard Service issue. Neither weapon was far from her hand at any given instant, though both were well out of sight to avoid startling the innocent members of the audience.

Tonight's crowd was their largest yet. In a way it was gratifying that Pias was able to attract so many people, but tonight it was merely an annoyance. If trouble were to break out, as they were almost positive it would, the large number of innocent bystanders would complicate the situation enormously. Yvette preferred to think of her job in terms of protecting the innocent rather than hurting them.

Pias was half an hour into his exhortation when the attack began. Yvette – whose eyes, as always, had been scanning the audience looking for any faint hint of trouble – detected a subtle motion three rows in front of her. One man, apparently listening with the same rapt attention as his neighbors, was reaching surreptitiously under his shirt. The movement was too slow, too calculatedly casual, to be the mere scratching of an itch.

There could still be a dozen different interpretations for the man's gesture, but Yvette had to put her intuition on the side of the worst possible one. 'Rube!' she shouted to warn her spouse. At the same instant, her stunner was in her hand and she was firing at the person who'd raised her suspicions.

She never did find out whether that particular man was a part of the conspiracy – but it is a fact that, at her shout, all hell broke loose in the auditorium. The man she'd shot slumped forward in his seat, unconscious for two hours – the effect of the number four stun Yvette had her weapon set for. But other guns seemed to sprout like mushrooms throughout the rest of the hall. At least six other people, as though on cue, rose from their seats, weapons in hand. Yvette's shout from the rear of the room had startled them, but they remained true to their original purpose and aimed their blasters at the figure on the stage.

Pias had been raised with a different heritage than Yvette. To him, the cry of 'Rube!' was just the meaningless utterance of a name, rather than the old circus battlecry of 'Hey Rube!' that had been abbreviated over the passage of centuries. Unlike a d'Alembert, he did not leap into instinctive action upon hearing that sound.

He was, though, very much on edge after the previous attempts on his life. He recognized Yvette's voice, and knew that she would not be yelling anything in the middle of his exhortation unless something was very wrong indeed. It was the cry itself, not its content or meaning, that prompted him to act.

In midstride and midsentence, he suddenly broke for the righthand side of the stage. The searing white light of blaster bolts was suddenly flashing out of the darkness toward him, and every move he made seemed much too slow. By the time he'd reached the end of the stage, his ministunner was in his hand and ready for use. He dived off the stage into the right-hand aisle, rolled, got to his feet and started running into the comparative darkness of the hall – straight into the teeth of danger.

The crowd, as was to be expected, flew into a panic at this unexpected display of violence. People looked around at one another dumbfounded, afraid. At the exhibition of blaster fire, several of the hysterical sorts began screaming at the top of their lungs. This only fueled the fire worse, of course. People began standing up to head quickly for the exits, regardless of the fact that such action put them directly within the line of blaster fire. Several people were cut down simply because they panicked and started to flee when they should have remained frozen in their seats until the shooting was over. Many other people were seriously injured in the general rush to evacuate the auditorium as quickly as possible.

Yvette managed to down two of the gunmen before the major panic made conditions too hectic to do much. She was, unfortunately, working against the flaws of her stunner, which was a limited weapon. Instead of simply being able to sweep across an area in a single beam like a blaster, a stun-gun shot out discrete charges, then required a fraction of a second to recharge before it could be fired again. Yvette's reflexes were faster than her weapon's, and it slowed her down.

The lighting technicians in the hall were just as startled and frightened as the audience. Instead of turning on the house lights, they simply deserted their posts and fled the building, leaving the majority of the auditorium in darkness. Pias, coming off the stage where lights had been shining in his eyes, had trouble adapting to the dimmer light in the aisle – but here the panic worked in his favor. So many people had stood up and tried to leave, jamming the aisle with their bodies, that the gunmen had no clear shot at him. The brief respite gave Pias's eyes time to adjust, after which he took a more active role in the proceedings.

Pias shrugged off the outer caftan that would only hamper his movements and pushed his way through the crowd in a relentless determination to get back at some of the men who'd been shooting at him. The audience's panic made his antagonists stand out all the more – they were the ones calmly holding their ground, weapons drawn and searching for him in the midst of the chaos. They were more visible than he was at the moment, though his bright white costume stood out from the people around him, and he was able to get off two good shots with his ministunner before being swept along with the tide of panicky people.

There were still a couple of blasterbats in the hall, but their position was becoming less tenable by the second. They had lost their primary advantage of surprise and secrecy, and still had failed to hit their target. Not only was this counselor able to fight back, but he had help from some very skilled person in the audience, who was picking them off cleanly. Now that all the spectators had bolted for the exits, their cover was gone, as well as a clear shot at their target. These men were not ordinary gangsters, with no concern for human life; they were religious zealots who wanted to rid the Galaxy of opposition to their beliefs. They still had strong moral principles, and firing their blasters into a crowd of innocent people just to kill one heretic went against their grain. They decided that the time had come to flee.

Almost as though they were of one mind, they left their stations and pushed their way through the screaming mob toward the side exits. Yvette first saw them go, and yelled to Pias, barely making herself heard over the din. Pias saw where she pointed, and nodded back at her. The two SOTE agents elbowed people aside as they pushed against the current, not toward the side door where the gunmen were going, but toward the front stage.

Once they were past the bulk of the mob they were able to move faster. The two blasterbats had disappeared out the

side door by now, which made speed all the more impera-
tive. The Bavols raced backstage, where they encountered
not a soul, and out the stage door. There were only a few
aircars on Purity, but Yvette and Pias, pulling rank by using
their code names Periwinkle and Peacock, had appropriated
one from the local SOTE office for just such a situation. This
one was not as fancy as the one Jules and Vonnie had with
them on Nampur, but it would serve its purpose.

The agents hurried inside their vehicle and Pias turned on
the antigrav. The aircar shot straight up into the sky, un-
mindful of any other air traffic; after all, a small town on
Purity didn't *have* any other air traffic. From their lofty
vantage point, Yvette and Pias could survey the scene
around the meeting hall with almost godlike objectivity.

In the darkness below they could barely make out the
shapes of the audience milling in confusion outside the auditorium. Moving at well over a hundred kilometers an hour
down the narrow streets of the village away from the hall
was a pair of headlights. Since mechanized traffic on Purity
was so slight, those lights could only represent the getaway
car being driven by the two escaping gunmen. Yvette
pointed, but Pias had already seen the lights and was flying
their car in that direction.

'Not too low,' Yvette cautioned him. 'We don't want
them to spot us. After all, we want them to get away.'

She smiled as she added, 'Or at least we want them to
think they did.'

CHAPTER TEN

AMBUSH UNDER THE SUN

The day after they arrived on Slag, Jules and Yvonne were to be shown how the base searched for its raw materials, and how those resources were mined and transported back to the plant for processing. George Chactan, their host, begged off from the trip, claiming he had important work to be done in his office; instead, he left them in what he assured them were the capable hands of his plant manager, Ray Furman.

Along with a crew of seven workmen, the d'Alemberts and Furman boarded a small rocketbus and began the long flight away from the base. The rocketbus was a small, box-carlike craft, operating on a combination of antigravity and rocket propulsion. It was basic transportation for use under conditions similar to Slag's, with few amenities available for its passengers. The rocketbuses in use here had been specially adapted for this environment, with a shiny exterior hull that reflected most of the searing radiation it received every second from the sun that hung motionless overhead.

Although they were completely enclosed within the rocketbus, everyone wore their spacesuits fully closed in case of accident. The spacesuits, too, were not the standard issue. The soles of the boots were triply reinforced and insulated against the rigors of Slag's heat. The exteriors were, like the hull of the rocketbus, highly reflective, and special design considerations had gone into ensuring that the cooling systems were as effective as Man knew how to make them. The helmet faceplates were extra thick and highly tinted to minimize the glare from the rocks all around.

One of the workmen piloted the craft, leaving Jules and Yvonne nothing to do but gaze out the window at the startling scenery below. Both d'Alemberts had visited airless worlds before – particularly Jules, who had done significant work on the moon Vesa – but they had never experienced anything quite like Slag.

It was a world of stark contrasts. Where the sunlight shone on bare rock, the glare was nearly blinding even through their dark faceplates. In places where the rocks cast shadows along the ground, the darkened area was pitch black, without hope of illumination. High, ragged chains of mountains shot up out of nowhere from barren plains whose floors were cracked and crisscrossed with crevices. Occasionally they could see silvery pools lying placidly like enormous globules of mercury. Temperatures could range from three hundred and fifty celsius in direct sunlight to minus two hundred and forty within the inky shadows.

As they passed over the ground, Yvonne spotted some machinery busily working below them. 'What's that?' she asked Furman, pointing out her window.

The plant manager leaned over to look. 'That's an automated mining station. Our geologists found a good surface vein of something there – I'm not precisely sure which station that is, so I can't say what it's mining. It digs up the ore, loads it into homing cargo rockets and sends it to the base. The rockets then return for another load.'

'Can we stop and see it?'

'There's really nothing to see. We're going to a site that has a little more potential, and we have to check it out to see whether it's worth putting an automated station there. That should give you a lot more to see. We'll be there in just a little bit.'

As Furman predicted, it was only a few minutes later that the rocketbus began settling toward the ground near some low hills. Their pilot was so skillful that they landed with but the gentlest of bumps. 'Ride's over,' Furman announced. 'Time to get to work. Everybody out.'

Even though their suits were well insulated, Jules and Yvonne experienced a psychological effect as they walked out into the bright sunlight, like walking into an oven. They knew better than to look straight up at the sun, which would have appeared to be the size of a large dinner platter held at arm's length; nonetheless, the temptation to peek at it, to view its corona and prominences with their own eyes, was a strong one. They had to content themselves with a look at the stars near the horizon in the daytime, spelling out unfamiliar constellations.

Furman's voice came over their helmet radios. 'Our geologists tell us that the vein we're looking for is at the base of those hills over there. Why don't we all go over and look?'

Jules and Yvonne began walking in the indicated direction, their boots crunching over the powdery surface. It was Jules who first noticed something was wrong, an itch at the back of his mind that things were not happening as they should. In a group of workers like this, under hazardous conditions, there was always a friendly banter, an undercurrent of conversation to help take their minds off the rigors they faced. He had seen plenty of it back at the base, both in the mess-hall-*cum*-recreation-room and in the factory area. The men were always joshing one another, making ribald comments, engaging in small talk about the most insignificant subjects to ward off the boredom that would otherwise set in on a lonely outpost planet.

Now the radio was completely silent. The only sounds he could hear were his own breath, the slight noises of nine other people breathing, and the sound of the blood rushing through his ears. He put a hand out to touch his wife's shoulder, cocking his head at a quizzical angle to ask in an unspoken way whether she thought anything strange was happening. The act of tilting his head let his eye catch a motion behind them, and he spun quickly around to see what was going on.

Furman and the seven workmen were grouped tightly together about ten meters back. All of them were armed with blasters, as were Jules and Vonnie; it had been considered prudent, since their partnership had not yet been fully confirmed. The motion Jules had caught out of the corner of his eye was Furman slowly reaching to his belt to grab the blaster he carried. Others of the men were reaching for their weapons as well.

At first, Furman froze when he saw Jules whirl quickly around to face him. Then, after a second's hesitation, he stopped trying to be secretive. There was no point in hiding his intentions any further. Pulling his blaster violently out of its holster, he aimed straight at the DesPlainians. 'Fire, men!' he ordered.

But that split second's delay had given the d'Alemberts time to start some action of their own. Seeing her husband's movement, Yvonne had also partially turned to find out what was happening behind them. Her mind was just as quick at assessing the situation as Jules's. 'Break!' Jules cried, giving her arm a slight push, and – seeing the drawn blasters in the workmen's hands – she needed no further instructions.

Bolts of potent energy leaped from the barrels of the enemy's blasters, but the targets were no longer where they'd been. The surface gravity on Slag was eighty percent of Earth normal – enough to make Furman and his cohorts feel livelier and a little faster than they normally would have, but not nearly fast enough to keep up with a pair of well-trained DesPlainians.

Jules and Yvonne were moving in opposite directions, so quickly that they seemed scarcely more than a blur to the men aiming at them. Jules was headed for the foothills a dozen meters away, hoping to find cover behind some rocks. The bulky spacesuit slowed him down a bit, even more so than normal because it was not the proper size; Vonnie and he were shorter and stockier than average, and the suits they'd been given were an awkward fit. Nevertheless, desperation lent extra speed to his feet, and Jules fairly flew across the open ground to the safety of the rocks. He was tempted, as the blaster bolts cleaved through the empty space he'd vacated, to make a long leap and dive behind the boulders, but he knew that would be a foolhardy maneuver. One tiny tear in his spacesuit would finish him just as surely as a dead hit by a blaster beam. He made it behind the rocks on his feet, then drew his blaster to return the others' fire.

Yvonne did not have as easy a time of it. There was no readily available cover in the direction toward which she broke when the trouble began. There were better than twenty meters of open ground to cover before she could reach the dark shadows of the range of hills – but once inside those shadows, even though there was nothing physical between herself and the gunmen, she would be reasonably safe. On an airless world like Slag there were no atmospheric particles to diffuse sunlight into places the sun itself did not reach. When an area was in shadow, it was totally black, and she would be completely invisible to the men standing in sunlight, while she'd be able to see them perfectly.

The problem, though, was living long enough to reach the shadowed area. Even as she sprinted for safety, Yvonne drew her blaster and fired a shot in the general direction of the men behind her. She was moving too fast to aim well, but the effort did remind them that they, too, were in an exposed position. A couple of them started to look for cover of their own, now that the ambush had failed to achieve its objective, and that gave Vonnie a few extra precious seconds.

Jules, seeing his wife's plight, was now in a position to help her. From the security of his hiding place, he fired out at the enemy grouped in the open. They had already started to break up and take cover after Yvonne's shot, so they were not quite as easy a target, but Jules was a crack shot. His beam hit one man dead center. There was a hissing sound through the radio receiver, and then a soul-shattering scream that died out quickly as the man's air supply rushed out of his suit through the hole the blaster bolt had left. A small cloud of vapor surrounded his spacesuit momentarily, then vanished as the oxygen molecules rapidly dissipated into the vacuum.

Jules's beam continued slashing outward, catching a second victim along the back of a leg. Although the wound would not have been fatal on most worlds, it was the hole burned in his spacesuit that killed the man. He died with the same scream of agony, the same cloud of rapidly dispersing gases as the first.

The rest of the men had, by now, managed to take cover, either behind scattered small rocks or alongside the rocket-bus itself. Vonnie, too, was now out of sight, hidden most effectively by the shadow in which she stood.

'Why the doublecross, Furman?' Jules asked over the suit radio. 'If we don't make a favorable report, our two organizations will never work together as partners.'

'It's hard to picture us working as partners with SOTE,

anyway,' Furman replied. 'Too many differences of opinion.'

Jules's heart sank. If his and Vonnie's cover as SOTE agents had been pierced, it would be impossible to talk their way out of the situation; all the forces at Chactan's disposal would be after them. Still, he had to try making one last attempt to continue his bluff. 'SOTE? I don't know what you're talking about. We hate them as much as you do.'

'We checked that list of "customers" you said you had. None of them exists anywhere except in SOTE's files – and not even there until you made the list up.'

Jules was certainly impressed with this gang's informational sources. He had expected them to need a week or better to track down that list and come to any conclusions; instead, they seemed to have the data almost instantly. Their intimate knowledge of what was in SOTE's files as well as in files elsewhere in the Galaxy, bespoke computer taps that rivaled those of the Empire.

He was trying hard to think of something to say that might salvage the situation, but Yvonne spared him the trouble. From the shadowed darkness, her blaster raked out at the men in hiding. Her beam caught one who'd been slightly careless, leaving his flank exposed; she had walked calmly through the darkness of her shadow, assured of invisibility, and gotten him from an unexpected angle. As her bolt continued to play across the open area, it hit the rock behind which another man was hiding. The rock shattered and flew apart, but the man behind it managed to escape uninjured. He fired quickly back into the shadow at the approximate point where Yvonne's shot had come from. The SOTE agent had to back away quickly to avoid being hit.

The enemy gunmen now unleashed their firepower into the shadowy area. Even though they couldn't see Yvonne, they knew she was in there somewhere, unprotected by rocks or other obstacles; if they played their beams throughout the area, they were bound to hit her. Jules realized that, too. Taking a deliberate risk, he stood up and sprayed them with fire of his own. The parched ground cracked and blew apart as the searing ray from his weapon burned across the landscape. The opponents ceased their shooting into the shadow as they had to cover themselves from the attack in the other direction, giving Yvonne more time to hide herself once again.

Jules ducked back down behind his rocks after accomplishing his objective of taking the fire away from his wife. 'It's a stalemate, Furman,' he said over the radio. 'We can keep trading shots back and forth all day without much result. We're going to have to come to some agreement.'

'We still outnumber you, five to two. You can't keep dodging all our beams forever.'

'It doesn't have to be forever,' Jules pointed out. 'All our oxygen tanks are the same size. I estimate we've got less than four hours apiece before they have to be changed, or we'll all die of asphyxiation.'

'There are more tanks inside the bus. We can get to that and you can't.'

In response to that, Jules fired a shot at the ground right in front of the bus's hatch. 'Anyone who tried won't live to make it inside. Care to risk it?'

There was silence from the other side for more than a minute as Furman thought over the possibilities. Jules was comforted by the knowledge that at least the other men could not be conferring on secret plans; they were so spread out that their only means of communication was via helmet radio, and the SOTE agents would be able to overhear everything they said.

At last Furman broke the stillness. 'Cover me, men,' he said. 'I'm going to try to make it anyway.'

White rays of intense energy poured out of the gunmen's barrels as the spacesuited figure of the plant's manager ran across the open ground to the bus. Jules tried to get a shot at him, but he was pinned down by fire from the workmen's blasters; there was no way he could reach a good shooting position without exposing himself to those deadly bolts. Yvonne, too, dared not shoot, lest she give away her position in the shadow. The DesPlainians could only watch helplessly as Furman reached the bus's hatch and dived inside safely.

'Khorosho, men, I did it, now it's your turn. Once we get in the bus, we can let them have this place if they like it so much. Or they can try to walk the three hundred kilometers back to the base.'

As a group, the four remaining gunmen broke from their hiding places and ran for the rocketbus. They tried to keep up their blaster fire as they did so, but it was harder for them to shoot and run at the same time, and they were not nearly as effective as they'd been before. Realizing that if they did not act now they would never have another chance, Jules and Yvonne began firing back at the fleeing figures.

Two of their shots hit home, and the men died sprawled out on the baked ground just a few meters short of their destination. But the other two men succeeded in reaching the hatch and climbing inside the bus. The instant they were in the door slammed shut, locking the agents out from their only mode of transportation.

Seconds later, the craft gave a slight shudder and began lifting soundlessly into the darkened sky. Jules and Yvonne, no longer fearing any blaster fire, raced out of their hiding places toward the spot where the craft had lain. Jules fired upward at the belly of the receding bus, hoping to hit something on the unshielded underside and disable the vehicle. Vonnie added her firepower to his, and the twin blaster beams scored the bottom of the rocketbus.

Nothing happened for several seconds, and the rocketbus lifted higher off the ground. It was at the very limit of effective blaster range when the continued beams from the d'Alemberts' weapons finally burned through the casing and hit some of the vital machinery. In this case, it was the antigravity generator that was most severely affected.

There was a flash of sparks and the bus suddenly lurched to one side. As the pilot – Furman, most likely – realized what had happened, he tried to compensate by firing the rockets on the other side. In his panic, he fired too long, and the vessel began to roll over, turning the antigravity field away from the body of the planet. With the field weakened by the damage to the generator and the ship no longer oriented in the proper manner, the antigrav drive could not keep the bus aloft. It began plummeting to the ground with all the grace of a dead condor. The pilot, in those last few seconds, tried several desperate maneuvers with the jets and the gyros, but to no avail.

The rocketbus hit the ground with a jolt the d'Alemberts could feel even through their thickly padded boots. It was a strange, silent crash with no explosion; the craft just caved in as though it had been made of wet cardboard, then lay deathly still on the bright plain of Slag.

Jules and Yvonne ran over to the wreck with guns drawn, just in case there might be some survivors – but there weren't. Looking at the twisted mass of metal, the agents knew that no living thing could have lived through a crash that bad. The wreckage was so badly mangled that there wasn't even any way to get inside without professional salvage equipment. Furman and his two remaining henchmen were undeniably dead.

The d'Alemberts stood silently beside the demolished bus, looking first at it, and then at each other. Both of them were fully aware how bad their situation was; no words could have expressed the desperation. They were stranded on the surface of the Galaxy's most hostile planet, three hundred kilometers from any occupied settlement. Their only means of transportation had been destroyed, and even if they could get back to the base they would be shot on sight. If they tried to walk back to the base across the blazing terrain, they would have to take into account the fact that they only had enough oxygen to last them four hours – and not even a DesPlainian could walk that fast!

CHAPTER ELEVEN

THE ARMY OF THE JUST

Pias and Yvette hovered leisurely above the town, looking down at the darkened streets. The groundcar driven by the fleeing gunmen was readily identifiable as a pair of headlights speeding along the road, the only motorized vehicle in the area. Groundcars, no matter how rapidly they were driven, were no match in a race with an aircar; Pias, in fact, had to hold down their air speed to a bare minimum to avoid overshooting their quarry. Other than that, he and his wife had little trouble keeping up with the men who had just tried to kill them.

If the fugitives knew they were being followed, they gave no indication. They traveled in the straightest possible course, with no attempt to elude possible pursuit. 'Amateurs,' Yvette remarked. 'They know how to fire a blaster, but they don't know the first thing about real undercover work. One of the first things they teach at the Academy is how to follow someone and how to know when you're being followed yourself. I really don't think we have much to worry about from their sort.'

'There are a lot of them, though, and they're well armed,' Pias reminded her. 'Their sheer force of numbers makes them dangerous.'

'And they do have that robot on their side. That worries me most of all.'

Below them, the groundcar had left the outskirts of the town behind it and was fleeing now through open countryside. After half an hour's fast drive, it pulled up in front of a small farmhouse, kilometers away from its nearest neighbors. 'Looks so quiet and innocent down there, doesn't it?' Pias commented.

'We'd better move in fast, before they have a chance to report to their headquarters about their failure at the hall. The more confusion we can sow at HQ, the better off we'll be.'

Obligingly, Pias dropped their vehicle silently to the ground, landing with a gentle bump a hundred meters from the farmhouse. The two agents leaped out from either side of the craft and ran toward the quiet building, stun-guns drawn. At Yvette's whispered instructions, Pias ran around to the far side of the house, while Yvette took up a station beside a window on the near side. She grabbed hold of the top of the window frame and waited for several seconds, giving her husband time to get into position. Then, pushing herself away momentarily, she swung back toward the window feet first. She dropped into the room amid a crashing of glass and drew her stunner once again.

Her entry had been Pias's signal. On the other side of the house she could hear another crash as the male half of the team also forced his way into the farmhouse. Yvette raced toward the center, knowing Pias would be doing the same. Somewhere, they would catch their enemies in the middle – not an enviable position to be in when such a highly trained team of SOTE agents was on the move.

The room Yvette found herself in was dark and empty. She crossed it quickly and opened the door to the central hallway. She was just in time to catch sight of a figure fleeing from a room on the other side of the house. On sheer reflex Yvette fired and the man dropped. The SOTE agent continued on into the room her victim had just left.

Pias, she found, had everything under control in here. Four bodies – three male, one female – were lying unconscious on the floor in undignified poses. They had been taken completely by surprise at the sudden entrance, and had no chance to reach for their own weapons before Pias downed them. Yvette's husband grinned as his wife raced into the room. 'Simple target practice,' he said. 'Not even moving targets, really, except for the one who ran out of the room. I presume you got him.'

'What about the rest of the house?'

The grin wavered on Pias's face. 'I haven't checked yet.'

'Then don't be so cocky,' Yvette lectured sternly. 'Always check to make sure you've gotten *everybody* before you relax.' She herself had made that mistake once, on a spaceliner en route to Vesa, and she still considered herself lucky to have survived it. If her voice sounded excessively harsh, it was because she loved her husband and did not want him killed because of some stupid blunder.

Pias looked hurt by Yvette's tone, but knew she was right. 'Yes, ma'am,' he said, saluting smartly.

The two agents separated once more and spread out to search the rest of the house. Yvette checked a couple of rooms and found them empty. The door to a room at the back was closed. Yvette hesitated for a moment, then kicked it in and backed off slightly. It was well that she did, as a blaster beam came sizzling through the air just centimeters in front of her nose.

Recovering her balance, she dived forward through the opened door, rolled and fired her stunner in the direction from which the blaster bolts had come. Her opponent had moved slightly himself, and her shot just missed. The blaster's beam came sweeping through the air in a deadly arc as she squeezed off a second shot. This time she hit her mark and the man dropped to the floor – but not before the leading edge of the blaster beam had touched her left shoulder. Yvette cried out and fell backward, avoiding more serious injury from the beam. Her shoulder burned like fire itself, even though she knew intellectually that it was a minor wound.

Pias was at her side in an instant. He had finished checking out his side of the house when he heard the crackling sound that he knew meant trouble. He kept his eyes scanning for any further ambushers, but there were none. 'Evie,' he said, kneeling beside his wife, 'are you badly hurt?'

'I'll be smooth,' she said, trying to give him a smile of confidence. 'You should see the other guy.'

Pias smiled back at her. 'Yeah, it takes more than a blaster to down a tough old battleax like you.'

'Is the house secure?'

'All smooth. I checked, this time.'

'*Bon*. Then help me to my feet. We've still got work to do and, pleasant though it is, I can't afford to just lie here in your arms all night.'

Yvette winced at the pain as Pias helped her up, but she made no sounds of protest. The old d'Alembert stoicism was coming to the fore, and she was certainly not going to let a little flesh wound prevent her from doing her job. She insisted on performing an equal share of the load as she and Pias hauled their captives all together into the first room and tied them up. By this time, the number three stuns the people had received were starting to wear off, and it was time to do some stern questioning.

This was Yvette's specialty. She had been trained in every form of the esoteric art of interrogation: verbal persuasion, psychological pressures, torture (which she preferred to call 'physical inducement') and drugs. She was a skilled practical psychologist, able to tell after only a few minutes which methods would be most effective on a given individual.

It was not hard to discover which of the captives was the leader – the others kept looking at the man named Hoyden whenever Yvette asked them anything, as though they were checking his reaction. None of them said much, which was about what Yvette had been expecting.

'They're all fanatics,' Yvette explained to Pias, rubbing her painful shoulder all the while. 'There's nothing worse than trying to break one of them. You can tear their bodies apart joint by joint and it only makes them feel more noble. Given plenty of time and the proper milieu I could work them down – but time is obviously limited. We want to strike further before Clunard realizes her plans against us have failed. I'll have to resort to the quick and dirty techniques.'

Pias knew exactly what she meant – nitrobarb. It was the only drug ever developed under which any subject was compelled to tell the complete truth, which would have made it an invaluable tool except for its side effects. Unfortunately, the drug had a fifty percent mortality rate, and this had led to its being banned throughout the Empire. Mere possession of it was a capital offense – but that did not stop people on both sides of the law from using it.

Yvette removed the tiny hyposprayer and vial of nitrobarb from the secret compartments in the heels of her shoes and administered the drug to Hoyden. Within half an hour he was powerless to resist her questioning, and told her everything she needed to know about the location and organization of the Army of the Just.

The army itself was encamped halfway around the world, on another continent altogether. The base was in a deep valley, heavily overgrown with vegetation so that it could not be spotted from space or from the air. All the recruits lived in a series of stark wooden barracks, under conditions that would have made the ancient Spartans seem profligate. They practiced discipline and various techniques of combat, and had at least two prayer sessions every day. They had a well-stocked arsenal built on one of the hillsides that surrounded the camp. Although they used all the latest advances in weaponry, they eschewed technology in general. From the way Hoyden talked, their fighting seemed to be on the level of the old Viking berserkers.

'They hardly seem like much of a threat to the Empire,' Pias remarked privately to Yvette. 'It would seem that a few well-trained battalions of Imperial Marines could wipe them out in under an hour.'

'Perhaps,' Yvette mused. 'But remember, you raised the question of their sheer numbers. Then too, they're all heavy-grav natives, far faster and stronger than most Imperial Marines. In a face to face confrontation, it's true that some strategically placed high-powered blasters could simply sweep across their ranks and decimate them – but remember, Lady A and her people will be planning their strategy, and I don't think they're stupid enough to put this army into a face to face battle. They're more likely to be used in spot fighting, where there aren't many Imperial Marines at the moment. An army like this could be landed at a chosen spot, devastate a city, and lift off for their next destination before the Empire can react. I suspect that's what the Head's worried about, and I know the thought bothers me.'

'*Khorosho*, then what do we do from here? Now that we know the location of the base, we can simply bomb the army into the ground.'

Yvette shook her head. 'The simplest solution isn't always the best. If the Clunard robot doesn't happen to be at the camp when we do the bombing, she'll just go on and start the whole process over again. We have to remember that she's the real enemy, not the members of the army. Most of them are honest people who've been misled by a maniacally clever traitor. I hate to kill them without reason. If we can eliminate the cause, the rest of the movement will wither away of its own accord.'

'Do we try tackling the army ourselves?' Pias asked. 'I admit we're a pretty good team, but even so I don't like the odds of several thousand against two.'

'We should reconnoiter, at least, look the army over for ourselves. Maybe then some idea will occur to us. And of course we'll have some back up. We can notify the local office exactly where the army is located, so that if anything happens to us they won't have to start from scratch again.'

'We'll have to do better than that,' Pias said. 'We'll be sure they have a team standing by, ready to blast in there and help if we get into any trouble.'

Yvette smiled. 'I always thought you were the brash, confident gambler. Has married life softened you, made you lose your nerve?'

'Not at all,' her husband smiled back. 'The smart gambler knows that you do everything possible to increase the odds in your favour before you even start playing the game. A successful gambler only bets on a sure thing.'

They notified the local SOTE office of the army's where-abouts and that they planned to conduct a little spying mission. The planetary chief assured them he would have the local forces standing by; at a prearranged signal broad-cast over their aircar's radio, his people would come in with blasters blazing, if necessary, to rescue these special agents. He also assured Yvette he would dispatch a team to the farmhouse to pick up the prisoners and hold them for further questioning.

With those details squared away, the Bavols took off on their long flight. If they'd had a spaceship available to them they could have made the journey in a single suborbital trip of only an hour or so; but Purity was a large planet and, despite their aircar's speed, it took them better than fourteen hours to reach their destination on the other side of the globe. They had to land carefully, a good distance away from the valley where the Army of the Just was camped so their vehicle would not be spotted. From that point they continued on foot up the hillside to a spot overlooking the valley.

It was early in the morning, local time, just a few hours before sunrise. There was a light snow on the ground, barely more than frost. Peering down into the gloom, the agents had to compliment Clunard on her plans – the camouflage was so perfect that, even knowing the base was there, they had a hard time spotting it. There was just the tiniest glimmering of light through the underbrush to indicate where the watchfires were burning.

'We'll have to move in closer,' Yvette said, rubbing her shoulder as she'd been doing frequently since they left the farmhouse. The burning pain had all but disappeared, to be replaced by a dull, throbbing ache that was almost as bad. 'We can't see anything significant from here.'

Pias nodded in the darkness and the two moved forward down the hill. The defenses around this camp were not as stringent as those Yvette's family had encountered around the terrorist camp on Glasseye, partly because the Army of the Just had done nothing overtly illegal yet and were not afraid of being hunted. Also, their numbers were sufficiently strong that they feared no local force. There were no metal detectors here, just routine sentry patrols that the Bavols easily evaded. Even so, the hill was steep and slippery with snow, and the climb was difficult, particularly for Yvette with her sore arm. It was almost sunrise as they reached the floor of the valley.

They decided this time to stay together rather than splitting up. They could only cover half as much territory this way, but in the event of trouble they would be able to fight as a team and thus have a better chance.

The valley floor was almost as thickly wooded as the hills surrounding it. There were no parade fields, no exercise grounds, no large open areas for combat maneuvers – nothing, in short, that would allow the camp to be spotted from the air. This army was not being trained according to traditional methods of combat, anyway; when they attacked, it would be with wide-angle blaster fire that did not require accurate aim or coordinated action. This was to be an army held together by the discipline and righteousness of its faith, an army of fanatics like a relentless, brutal machine, smashing all before it that did not agree with its stern principles.

The barracks were lined up in two rows down the center of the camp. They were of unpainted wood with crude thatched roofs, emphasizing the stark severity of Clunard's philosophy. Each building was thirty meters long and ten wide, and there must have been at least fifty of them stretching off to the far side of the valley. According to the instructions posted on them, the barracks were strictly segregated according to sex; Pias mused that this was one of the few armies in human history without camp followers, racy language or drunken, bawdy songs. Pias privately doubted whether such an army would be able to withstand a long, drawn-out campaign – but, as Yvette had pointed out, they could do immense damage in the short period of time they would actually be used.

They sneaked up alongside one of the buildings and peered in through a window at the sleeping figures. Both of them were aghast at the living conditions inside. Bunks were piled four high to the ceiling, with but the narrowest of aisles between one stack and the next. There was no room for privacy, no room for comfort of any sort.

'I've seen fancier flophouses,' Yvette whispered as they backed away into the underbrush once more. 'They must have at least two hundred men crowded in there. That would mean something like ten thousand in the entire camp.'

'It probably gets them in the proper mood,' Pias observed. 'If I had to live under conditions like that, I know I'd be fighting mad.'

They checked a few of the other buildings at random and found conditions similar to the first. The sky was beginning to lighten, now, though the sun itself had yet to climb over the tall hills. Realizing that they had to hurry before they were caught in full daylight, the two SOTE agents quickened their pace of observation. They gave the armory a quick check. This was another crude building of the same style as the barracks but considerably bigger. It was built right against the side of one hill, with three guards standing duty out front.

There were the beginnings of movement through the camp now as the cooking personnel prepared the daily breakfast. Pias and Yvette had to move extra carefully to avoid detection. Soon the entire army would be awake and bustling about on their daily chores, and the SOTE team's spying would be effectively curtailed. They had to make the most of their few remaining minutes.

'Let's see if we can find the Administration Building,' Yvette suggested. 'Anything we can get there is bound to be some help.'

They slipped around the perimeter of the compound, two more moving shadows in the emerging dawn. They passed the Mess Hall and the Prayer Hall before finally reaching the building they were seeking. Like all the other structures in the camp, this was merely a crude wooden shack, unpainted except for the stenciled letters identifying its function.

There were two women standing guard out in front of the building, but the back windows were totally unsecured. After checking one room to make sure it was empty, Pias pried open the window and the two agents slipped inside to continue their investigation.

They had their stunners drawn, and it was a lucky thing. They had just emerged from the room they'd entered and were starting down the hallway when a party of three people emerged from a doot at the far end – Clunard's aide Elspeth FitzHugh and two others. They were startled at the sight of the intruders and tried to draw their sidearms, but the Bavols, who'd been expecting possible trouble, were faster. Their stun-guns buzzed and the three at the other end dropped to the floor. They would be out for two hours from the number four charges.

Yvette cursed. 'I'd wanted to do this without leaving any trace.' Even as she spoke, she and Pias started moving quickly down the hall to investigate the room from which the enemy trio had emerged.

'Almost impossible in a place as crowded as this,' Pias consoled her. 'Relax; we'll find what we can and be away before they have a chance to get organized. Oof! This Fitz-Hugh's heavier than she looks.' He helped Yvette drag the three bodies into an empty office and closed the door. With their victims out of sight, it would be a while yet before anyone knew of their presence here.

They were in luck – the office from which FitzHugh and the others had come was Tresa Clunard's personal headquarters. Though as spartan in its decor as the rest of the camp, there was still an aura of power to it, the feeling that decisions affecting many lives were made in here all the time. 'Jackpot!' Pias whispered. 'Let's take all we can get and sort it out later.'

Each had a miniaturized camera tucked into his pocket, and they started snapping pictures of every document in sight. There were several bookreels with coded labels; Pias pocketed them in the hope they might contain revealing data about the Army of the Just. They rifled quickly through desk drawers and pried open locked filing cabinets in hopes of getting the vital clues they needed.

So intent were they about their business that they didn't hear the sounds of approaching footsteps until it was almost too late. Yvette spun, stun-gun in hand, just as the doorknob began to turn. Pias was a tiny fraction of a second slower, but the angle at which he was standing in relation to the door gave him the better shot.

The door opened and Tresa Clunard stood there, just as surprised as the SOTE agents she'd interrupted. Although he knew the effort would be wasted against the robot, Pias's reaction was instinctive. His finger tightened on the firing button of his stunner even as he wished he'd pulled his blaster instead.

The buzzing from the stun-gun filled the room, and Tresa Clunard slumped to the floor.

Pias and Yvette looked almost as stunned at the results of their actions as their victim had been. Clunard was a robot, and a stun-gun should not affect her. Was she playing dead, trying to trick them into tipping their hand? But what would be the point of that?

Pias drew his blaster and kept it trained on the still figure lying on the floor while Yvette approached it slowly. Kneeling down, she felt Clunard's pulse then, on impulse, took a small pin from a map on the wall and pricked the counselor's finger.

A drop of blood oozed through the tiny opening.

Tresa Clunard was not the robot they had fought that night in the dark. But who was?

CHAPTER TWELVE

A SAUNTER THROUGH HELL

The immensity of their predicament beat into Jules's and Yvonne's brains. They were stranded in an environment as hostile as any the mind of Man could comprehend, with a limited amount of oxygen and no transportation. Short of shooting themselves immediately, there seemed little they could do to avoid a lingering death on the surface of this aptly named slag heap.

It was Vonnie who broke the silence and broached the question. 'What do we do now?'

Jules looked around them – at the wreck of the rocketbus, at the bodies strewn over the landscape. 'The first thing,' he decided, 'is to get ourselves a little more air, which means more time. I don't think those fellows will be needing their tanks any more.'

He walked over to one body and inspected the oxygen tanks. Even though the suit had been burned open by the d'Alemberts' blaster and the gas within it had escaped into the vacuum of Slag's surface, the tanks were still doing their job, releasing their contents at a precisely measured rate. Jules turned off the valves and the flow stopped.

'We've got a lot more air than we first thought,' Jules said, looking at the five bodies sprawled on the ground. 'I'd estimate another twenty hours total, or ten more apiece in addition to our present four.'

'Fourteen hours,' Vonnie said slowly. 'It's better than four, but it's still not enough to get us home. The base is three hundred kilometers away.'

She and Jules were walking briskly among the corpses, turning off the oxygen tanks as they pondered their situation. 'We might wait for them to come to us,' Jules suggested. 'Chactan will be listening back at the base for word from his men about how the ambush went. When he doesn't hear anything he'll get anxious; he may even send out another rocketbus to investigate.'

'*Eh bien*, and what will they find when they get here? Five dead bodies sprawled out on the ground and us standing around waiting to be picked up. Try again, *mon cher*.'

'We hide the bodies and stand in the shadow so they can't see us.'

'We can't hide the rocketbus, darling. The crash is all too obvious.'

Jules turned off the last dead man's tanks as he paused to consider his wife's argument. 'And you think they'd prefer to leave well enough alone rather than land and try to rescue any possible survivors. That way they could be sure we were dead, even if it cost them a few men of their own.' Jules sighed. 'You're probably right. Whatever Chactan has flowing through his veins, I doubt it's the milk of human kindness. That leaves us right back at our original problem. There is no way we can walk three hundred kilometers in only fourteen hours.'

Yvonne suddenly stiffened and straightened up. 'How about twenty kilometers?' There was an edge of excitement in her voice.

'Easily. But what good will that do us?'

'Remember as we were flying here, we passed over that automated digging station. Furman commented that it dug up the ore, put it in homing cargo rockets and sent it back to the base. I'm not sure exactly how far back that was, but I don't think it could have been more than twenty kilometers. It was only a couple of minutes before we landed here.' Her voice was positively ecstatic now.

Jules caught her enthusiasm. 'We can hijack one of those homing rockets and use it to get us back to the base. We may have just enough time. Of course,' he added, trying to keep his excitement under control, 'the instant they spot us there it'll be all out warfare.'

'Do I have to come up with everything? I thought of this plan; I'll leave the problem of the base to you when we get there.' She put a slight emphasis on the word 'when'. 'In the meantime, shall we go for a little stroll? It's the perfect day for it – the sun is shining, the sky is clear. There would be birds singing in the trees, if there *were* any birds or trees, or any air for them to sing in.' She reached out and took her husband's gloved hand in her own and gave it a squeeze for luck.

They stayed around just long enough to remove the vital air tanks from the dead men's suits and strap them loosely around their own shoulders for future use. They conferred for a moment on which direction they had come from, and agreed that it must have been over that range of hills on their right. With those details taken care of, there was no further need to remain at this spot, and they began their long trek across the barren landscape.

At first, in an effort to make their trip as short as possible, they took long loping strides, as only a person from a three-gee world on a point-eight-gee world could take. They covered almost a kilometer across open ground in this manner before they had to stop it. The extra air tanks they had strapped around them kept banging their bodies awkwardly, and their suits' cooling systems, which had already had to work hard under the harsh glare of Slag's sun, had been strained to near the limit by their exertions during the shoot-out. These long, graceful leaps of theirs brought the suits right to the tolerance point. The agents found their faceplates fogging up with the moisture of their own breath and sweat, and the heat inside the suits building to uncomfortable levels. Realizing that they still had a long distance to cover, they decided it would be wiser to pace themselves at a more reasonable rate. There would be time enough to reach the digging station even if they kept themselves to a normal walk.

To save their suits from further strain during what they knew would be a long and arduous ordeal, they did as much walking as they could in the coldness of shadows, holding hands to avoid losing one another in the pitch darkness of those shaded areas. Even this solution had its drawbacks, however; Vonnie walked straight into a rock that had lain unseen in her path, and would have been sent sprawling had not Jules's strong grip pulled her back and kept her on her feet.

The patches of shadow were comparatively rare, though, on this open plain. For the most part they walked under the full heat of the blazing sun. They left a small trail of slowly settling dust in their wake, and their thickly insulated boots crunched over the dry, crumbly soil. The ground and the rocks reflected the killing heat back at them; it seemed almost as though they were at the focus of a telescope mirror. Even though the temperature inside their suits remained within comfortable limits, the DesPlainians could imagine only too well the temperatures around them.

To take their minds off their psychological discomfort, they talked a bit about the case, analyzing the situation and discussing alternative plans for what to do once they reached the base. Jules, though, was more concerned with the larger aspects of the situation.

'Chactan can't be the top man in this scheme,' he reasoned. 'He doesn't have the authority to establish a base here, not on a planet in an entirely different solar system from his native world.'

'Does he even need any authority? This is an unclaimed, undeveloped world. While it belongs to the Emperor by the simple fact of its being within the borders of the Empire, there is technically no one who *controls* it.'

'There are plenty of technicalities that go by the board in this Galaxy. There is an inhabited planet in this system, Tregania. If you were the duchess there, you'd keep an eye on all the worlds in your system, for your own peace of mind if nothing else. With so many terrorist gangs springing up all of a sudden, a world like Slag could harbor a viper very near your bosom, *n'est-ce pas*? Yet there is the base, right out in the open, apparently unconcerned that it might be spotted by some ducal patrol ship. That strikes me as strange, to say the least.'

'You think the Duke of Tregania is in on this conspiracy, then?' Vonnie had met only a couple of dukes in her life, one of them being her new father-in-law, and their trustworthiness had been beyond question. Although she knew that was not universally the case, she was still reluctant to believe that anyone who ranked that highly in the aristocracy would be willing to betray it.

Detecting the doubts in his wife's tone, Jules hedged. 'Not necessarily him, but it would almost have to be someone high on his staff. Someone has to give the local police orders not to investigate any goings-on here, and be able to cover up the facts if the base should accidentally be spotted. It could only be a top-ranking police official or a member of the Duke's council. But we can't rule out the Duke himself just because of his title. Remember, Duke Fyodor of Kolokov was a full participant in this conspiracy – and we netted nearly forty dukes and duchesses in the Banion affair. To some of these people, having power only increases their appetite for more; if they can't get it from the Emperor in a legal way, they'll go to someone else who'll promise them a better deal, no matter how treasonous it is.'

Two hours of walking brought them to the base of the hills that lay between them and the digging station. The range of hills extended as far as they could see in either direction, ruling out any thought of going around. There simply wasn't the time. The hills looked to be less than a kilometer high at the tallest point, and the D'Alemberts were in good physical condition. There appeared to be no insurmountable difficulties involved.

On Slag, though, nothing was quite as simple as it seemed. The DesPlainians discovered that, although the gloves of their spacesuits had been padded to allow them to handle objects on the surface, the gauntlets could not be padded nearly as thickly as the soles of the boots; otherwise the fingers, palms and wrists would not be able to bend well enough to be of any use. Holding onto any rock for more than ten seconds allowed the rock's heat to soak through the pads and begin burning their hands.

The climb was steep, and much more difficult than they'd expected. There was no wind or rain on Slag to erode the surfaces of the rock, to smooth them down and make them more gentle for climbers. Jagged escarpments rose above the agents as they ascended, some offering few handholds. In some instances, the rock projections were so sharp that they threatened to cut right through the material of the space-suits, which would have had fatal consequences. The d'Alemberts had to learn quickly not to put their full weight on any grip, and not to linger too long in one place lest they burn their hands. Several times the route they took upward proved to be impassable, and they had to work their way down again and look for another path to the top.

They were torn between the conflicting desires for both

speed and caution. Every second's worth of oxygen was beyond price, and they dared not waste their time with needless safeguards. At the same time, they had none of the standard safety equipment climbers normally carried – ropes, pitons, etc. – and a single slip could send them tumbling down onto some jagged outcrop of rock that would slice their suits open, killing them instantly. Physical exertion was not their problem, but they were sweating profusely nonetheless from sheer tension.

They had made it only halfway up the slopes when the air in their present tanks began running out. They found a firm outcropping on which to rest and changed to new sets of tanks, leaving the discarded old ones as eternal reminders of the two human beings who had once passed this way. On the surface of Slag, those containers would remain until the sun above went nova and swallowed the planet to which it had given birth.

They made it to the top of the ridge and took a second's rest to survey the journey ahead of them. On this side, the hills sloped downward less steeply, but with ominous series of deep ridges gouging through the range at irregular intervals. Jules and Yvonne discussed between themselves the best route to take to avoid those chasms.

'Look!' Vonnie pointed. Far away, across the plain at the base of another set of hills, was a small dot. 'That's the digging station, I'm sure of it.'

'It better be,' Jules said. His voice was even, but Yvonne could sense the tension behind it .'We don't have the oxygen to try climbing past that next range of hills as well.'

Climbing down was in some ways even more hazardous than climbing up, because they had gravity pulling in the same direction they were moving. If their hand- or footholds were not secure, they would find themselves falling, with tragic consequences.

At one point, Jules found himself lowering his feet into a silvery puddle. It had looked deceptively gentle, but the instant his boots entered the liquid there was a burning that scorched right through the suit material. He cursed and hurriedly pulled himself out, inspecting the damage ruefully.

Both his boots were covered up past the ankles with a bubbling gray liquid. He yowled in pain and Vonnie, who was just to his side and slightly above him, turned her attention his way. 'What is it?'

'I stepped in a pool of something molten. I'm not sure what, exactly.'

His wife bent down to give it a closer examination. 'Offhand, I'd say it was lead. It's starting to solidify, too.'

True enough, the molten lead – now in contact with the comparatively cooler surface of the spacesuit – was rapidly cooling into a solid coat on Jules's boots. The transference of heat was being conducted through the fabric of the boots to Jules's feet and legs. Without the suit, his feet would have been burned completely off; with it, he was merely in an agony comparable to a very bad sunburn.

'Will you be able to move on?' Vonnie asked.

'I'll have to, won't I?' But Jules's body belied the courage of his words. He tried to stand on his own and screamed from the pain.

'Here, darling, put your arm around my shoulder,' his wife said. 'We're almost down to the plain. We'll just have to watch where we step from now on, that's all.'

Vonnie's estimate of the distance turned out to be overly optimistic; it took them another couple of hours before they reached the bottom of the range of hills, and by that time they had had to shed air tanks once more. They now had just under six hours left in which to get back to the base and replenish their air supply.

Jules gazed out across the horizon at the tiny speck they hoped was the digging station. 'That's a long way for me to limp in a short time,' he said wistfully.

'Whoever said I was going to let you limp, lummox?' Yvonne said, stooping over. 'Climb on. My husband rides first class.'

'Vonnie, I couldn't . . .'

'Nonsense. You never objected to riding me before. Besides, the gravity's so light here that the two of us and our suits combined weigh less than I do normally back home on DesPlaines. Nothing to it. Now climb aboard.'

Jules did as he was told, hooking his arms and legs around her to hang on. The distribution of the weight was different than what she was used to, but it took only a small adjustment for Yvonne to compensate. The extra mass caused some inertia problems getting started that she hadn't expected, but once she was in motion it felt as though she were strolling through the *Bois Mercredi* back home with a knapsack on her back.

The molten lead on Jules's boots was hardening now into a tough metallic coating; the actual heat had stopped as the temperature equalized inside and outside the boots, but the burning pain in Jules's feet remained. 'You won't be able to run quite as fast with your boots coated with lead,' Yvonne remarked lightheartedly as she walked. 'I think you're about to get a new nickname: Leadfoot.'

Jules's response was unprintable.

The ground over which Yvonne walked was cracked and hard, an uneven surface unwilling to concede anything to the DesPlainian's indomitable courage. The weight of Jules on her back was not burdensome – as she'd said, the total of their combined weights was less than her own weight on her native world – but the distribution of the weight was awkward. She had to continually be leaning forward to avoid becoming unbalanced, producing a strain on her back and shoulders. They could both tell that she was breathing harder, using up her precious supply of air that much more quickly.

It seemed like ages before their destination became anything more than a mere speck on the horizon. Finally Jules's sharp eyes could detect a glint there brighter than the natural color of the rocks around them – the reflection of brilliant sunlight off the polished metal surface of the automated digging station. A moment later Vonnie spotted it, too, and her pace quickened in an effort to reach the station before too much more of their air was gone.

Soon they could make out more than just the glint of the metal as the station's shape became clearer. It was a collection of long, spidery legs on either side of a central axis. The multitudinous legs kept the machine stable while digging drills and shovels were constantly working at the ground underneath, loosening the desired material and loading it onto a conveyor belt that ran the length of the station's axis. The conveyor belt dumped its material into a large bin at the back end of the station; the bin itself was detachable, and, when full, would empty itself into the drone rocket that carried the ore back to the base for processing. Sticking up from the back of the digging station and shading most of the area was an enormous solar umbrella, its surface completely covered with photocells. The digging station would continue to operate as long as the sun itself kept shining down. When it ran out of ore beneath its present location, the legs would simply move it a few dozen meters away and the process would begin all over again. The series of deep trenches cut into the ground all around the station testified to the length of time it had been working in this area.

It was, of course, the drone rocket in which Jules and Yvone had the most interest. It took them longer to reach than they thought at first because they had to climb into and out of a series of deep trenches dug previously by the machine. Vonnie was sweating strenuously now, and her suit was barely adequate to the task. Already the edges of her faceplate were fogging over again with the moisture from her perspiration.

Finally they climbed out of the last trench and there before them, fifteen meters away, was the drone rocket. The fatigue suddenly lifted from Yvonne and she walked toward the rocket with renewed vigor.

It was a simple device lying horizontally behind the digging station, little more than an open tube with rocket engines on the back and a guidance system in the nose. It was about twelve meters long and four in diameter; the cargo hatch stood ajar, waiting for the station's bin to drop in its loads of ore. Being on Yvonne's shoulders already gave Jules an advantage for climbing up onto the rocket and looking down into the hold.

'It's almost empty,' he said, not even bothering to hide the disappointment in his voice. 'We must have just missed a full one taking its load back.'

'We can't just sit around here and wait for this one to fill up,' Vonnie said. 'That could take hours, or even days.' What she did not bother to say – they both knew it only too well – was that they only had less than two hours of air left in their tanks.

Jules was not about to give up. Leaning back down from the top of the missile, he helped Yvonne climb up there beside him. 'There's got to be some trip-gauge,' he mused aloud, 'some automatic register that tells the rocket when it's full. Then the door will close automatically and the rocket will head back to the base. All we have to do is find that and convince the ship it's got a full load.'

The two agents lowered themselves into the cargo hold and began their exploration of the interior. The logical place to look for the control was near the top, where the ore would be piled when the hold was filled. Jules once again climbed atop his wife's shoulders and they moved slowly around the nearly empty chamber, scanning the walls intently for an indication of anything that might be the control they sought.

After ten minutes their search was successful. Jules located the little mechanism, a simple device that pressed against the forward bulkhead, closing an electrical connection. Under normal conditions, the contact would not be made until the hold was so full of rock that it pushed against the top, but Jules could duplicate that effect by hand. 'Here goes,' he said, pushing the contact lever.

The result was all they could have hoped for. Above them, the cargo hatch swung ponderously shut, sealing them in total darkness within the missile. Jules climbed down from his wife's shoulders and the two of them braced themselves against the missile's rear wall. A few moments later they felt the walls begin to shake and a sudden pressure pushing them backward. Their rocket was homeward bound.

CHAPTER THIRTEEN

STANDOFF

With the discovery that Tresa Clunard was not the robot they sought, Pias and Yvette realized that once again they had badly miscalculated in evaluating their enemy. It had seemed so logical that the rapidly moving female shape they'd seen in the darkness at Clunard's headquarters would *be* Clunard that they hadn't stopped to analyze further. Now they would have to think extra fast to make up for their earlier mistake.

Yvette raised her head and looked about, as though just noticing something. 'Listen,' she whispered.

'I don't hear anything.'

'That's the problem – neither do I. The camp was on the verge of waking up when we came in here, and we've been here quite a while. Reveille should have blown by this time. Something has changed the camp's routine, and I don't like what that implies. Let's get out of here, *vitement* – and don't hesitate to use blasters.'

As it was, their action was barely in time. They came racing out of the administration building to find the structure almost completely surrounded by an advancing squadron of armed guards. The instant they were spotted, the two agents found blaster beams sizzling all around them. They returned the fire with beams of their own, forcing the attackers to break for cover. The Bavols did the same.

They used the layout of the camp itself to their advantage. There was an overgrowth of vegetation throughout the area to help camouflage it; that same underbrush helped hide them as they reached away from the scene of their near-entrapment.

All around them, the general alarm was sounding. Now that there was no longer the chance to take them by surprise, the army's security forces chose to rely on their superior numbers to capture and/or kill these intruders.

Thousands of fighters, primed for action ever since coming to this camp, poured out of their barracks like ants defending their hive. Loudspeakers all over the base blared that a pair of enemy agents had infiltrated the camp and were to be destroyed on sight.

If the Army of the Just had been trained according to standard military discipline, the Bavols would have been doomed. Fortunately for them, this army had been intended to fight as individual berserkers rather than as a coordinated unit. They were filled to overflowing with energy and enthusiasm, but little sense of teamwork. Even without a clear idea of what they were after, they started firing their blasters at random into the forest, burning down anything that moved – and occasionally hitting some of their fellow Puritans as well as starting small fires in the brush around the camp.

Pias and Yvette picked their way carefully through the confusion. Although the search for them was less than optimum, the enemy was present in such overwhelming numbers that there was always the fear a random shot might hit true. 'If we could make it back to our aircar,' Pias gasped as he ran alongside Yvette, 'we could send for reinforcements. The Service has its people all ready to jump in and bail us out.'

In answer, Yvette merely pointed at the sky. The army had mobilized some of its mechanized units, with several aircars already aloft and scanning the ground below. 'They'd see us going over the hill,' she said. 'And they'll spot our car soon enough, anyhow. We'd never reach it.'

Pias stopped for a moment, standing still in the midst of confusion. 'So what are we supposed to do, then? Run in circles around the bottom of this valley, hoping to tire out ten thousand soldiers by ourselves?'

'At this point, I'm not fussy. I'll listen to any reasonable alternative.' Yvette stopped, too, brushing her hair out of her face and looking at her husband with an inquisitive expression.

Pias closed his eyes for a second and took a deep breath. 'When in doubt, bluff,' he said. 'Get out your stunner again and follow me.' Opening his eyes once more, he led the way in a new direction through the forest. Wondering what he was up to but too out of breath to ask, Yvette could only follow after him and hope her Gypsy lord had not snapped a gear in his mental processes.

After a moment, his direction became clear. He was moving toward the one area where there was no shooting – and for good reason. The camp's armory was directly in front of them, and a few misplaced blaster beams could conceivably blow the entire valley into a fine powder.

They stopped right at the edge of the brush to give the armory a quick scan before going in. The three guards they had originally seen had been supplemented by two more, all standing out of stun-gun range from where the Bavols were now hiding. The agents would have to expose themselves before they could hope to down their opponents.

'We have an old saying on Newforest,' Pias explained breathlessly. ' "Better to bargain with borrowed goods." We'll be in a better position to negotiate if we hold a power equal to theirs. If they have more people, we'll have more firepower.'

This is madness, Yvette thought, but knew that only inspired madness had any chance of saving them now. 'You're a fool, and I love you!' She gave him a quick kiss on the cheek and raced out into the open facing the guards. Pias, a little startled by her bravado, was nonetheless just a step behind her.

The guards were understandably nervous that two people should come charging out of the bushes like lunatics, yelling and screaming and firing their weapons indiscriminately with the armory right there. It took an extra second to recognize that it was only stunners, not blasters, the two were firing, and thus they were posing no immediate threat to the weapons cache behind them. The guards were only armed with stunners, too – there had been no sense in tempting Fate with weapons of higher potency in such a dangerous area – and their guns had no greater range than the Bavols'. Both sides had to wait until the gap between them had narrowed before they could expect to hit anything.

The odds were five against two, but those two were far better trained, better prepared and more highly motivated than their opposition. Their lives were at stake, while to the guards it was merely a job. The SOTE agents moved so quickly that the guards could not get a clear shot at either of them. The Bavols' accuracy, on the other hand, was perfect.

The five guards fell to the ground and the agents rushed inside the rickety building, just as a group of pursuers burst from the bushes behind them. A couple of the soldiers raised their blasters to shoot the fleeing pair, but their squad leader brought them up short. 'Are you crazy?' he shouted. 'If you miss, the whole valley will blow up.'

By that time, Pias and Yvette had made it safely inside the building. They kept their stunners at the ready, but apparently there were no more guards inside. 'We've got them off balance for the moment,' Yvette said as she gulped in deep lungfuls of air. 'What happens now?'

'Now we get a few moments' respite while they check with whoever's in charge. In the meantime we have to prepare our bluff. Help me rig a dead man's switch attached to some of these explosives. We'll have to make them think seriously before attacking our position.'

Yvette was the more experienced of the pair at dealing with munitions, so she ended up doing most of the work. Her wounded left shoulder was bothering her again; during the brief chase she had managed to ignore the pain, but it was returning now with a vengeance. She pushed herself to the limit anyway; they had to work quickly before the army could regroup.

The dead man's switch they rigged took the form of a rope over a pulley. Pias held one end, while the other end was weighted. If he were to be shot, his hand would let go of the rope, the weight would fall and several tons of explosives would be ignited within this confined area. 'Now we'll see how good they are at gambling,' Pias remarked. 'The odds are just about even.'

'But what can we gain?'

'Time, if nothing else. We'd be dead by now if we hadn't ducked in here. Be thankful for small favors.'

They had barely finished rigging the switch when a party of soldiers burst into the armory, carrying stunners. They hesitated momentarily when they saw the unusual contraption the intruders had rigged, which gave Pias a chance to speak up. 'I'd advise you to point those things in some other direction,' he said. 'If I'm knocked unconscious and let go of this cord, Purity will have an enormous bomb crater to add to its list of scenic wonders – not that any of us would be around to enjoy it.'

The soldiers looked back and forth among themselves, wondering whether this crazy intruder was bluffing and not daring to take the risk. The man in front, who must have been the leader of the group, finally spoke. 'What do you want?'

Pias smiled. For the moment, the game was his. 'A broad philosophical question indeed,' he said, 'but one that indicates more of a cooperative spirit than you previously exhibited. For the beginning, let us say I want a bullhorn so that I may communicate with your high command over a long distance. One of you may go fetch it for me and the rest of you are to leave in as orderly a manner as you can arrange.'

The soldiers stood where they were, unsure of exactly what to do. Their orders had been to come up here and deal with the spies; they had probably even been willing to die in the attempt. But they could not take the responsibility for blowing up the entire camp in the process, and they had no way to judge how serious this young man was about his threat.

'I'd suggest,' Pias said after a pause, 'That you leave at once.' He gave the rope a shake to scare them, and the soldiers took the hint. They left quickly.

'That worked for now,' Yvette said, 'but how much longer can we go on bluffing?'

'Long enough – I hope. Just pray my arm doesn't get tired.'

'They can outlast us. All we have in here are weapons and explosives, no food. They could try starving us out.'

'They'll bring us food if I tell them I'm about to faint from hunger.'

Yvette looked at him seriously. 'Are you really prepared to go through with the bluff? It may come down to that.'

'We have our orders to break up this army somehow. I admit the Head wanted it done a bit more quietly – but if we can't get out of this with our lives, at least we can go knowing we've accomplished our mission. I have no intention of dying without good purpose. You're damn right I'll go through with it.' He sighed. 'If only we knew who the robot was ...'

'It's got to be the assistant, Elspeth FitzHugh,' Yvette said. 'She's the only other high-ranking female in this organization.'

'But we got her with a stunner just a few minutes ago in the administration building and she went down with the other two. The robot back in God's Will City wasn't even slowed down by a stunner.'

'The circumstances were different. It was completely dark back at the city headquarters raid. The robot knew we wouldn't be able to identify it, so it didn't mind betraying itself in an attempt to destroy us. Jules and I fought one in the dark on Ansegria, and it behaved the same way. But as soon as there was a chance it might be discovered, it ran away. It knows that its best weapon is to keep its identity totally secret.'

'Then it was faking today when we shot it,' Pias continued the reasoning. 'I thought it felt too heavy when I dragged it into the other room.'

Yvette nodded. 'It knew we'd be able to see it, so it pretended to succumb like the others and wait until we had left before sounding the alarm. It could see we were armed with blasters today, and that one of us could probably have destroyed it before it could act. It places survival and secrecy above everything else.'

The female agent shook her head, now, as though trying to clear it of a mental fog. 'If I weren't so damned stupid, I should have seen it was FitzHugh rather than Clunard right away.'

'What do you mean? And how dare you call the woman I love stupid?'

Yvette smiled in spite of herself. 'There's a pattern to the way these robots are being used. They're never the star of the picture, never the one on whom all attention is focused. That might give them away. Instead, they're someone at the side, someone few people would notice but who will be there when needed. The conspirators didn't try to duplicate the Princess, just the man they'd hoped to make her husband. When that didn't work, they had a duplicate of Lady Blood-star all ready to step in, to be an important member of the wedding party, but not the one in the spotlight. Now in this conspiracy they wouldn't pick Clunard, the star attraction who's standing in front of large crowds every night; instead, they'd go for little, unnoticed Elspeth FitzHugh, who just happens to be the top assistant and who keeps the entire operation running smoothly. The robots are content to be out of the limelight, but having the power nonetheless.'

The discussion was interrupted by the return of one of the soldiers with the bullhorn Pias had requested. Pias thanked the man, then told him to leave, with the added stipulation that he tell Sister Elspeth to begin negotiations via bullhorn. The man left quickly; the farther he was from the armory and the suicidal spies, the more comfortable he would feel.

A few minutes later, the voice of Elspeth FitzHugh boomed up the hill at them. 'Counselor Hanrahan, you and your wife must surrender immediately,' she said. 'We have you completely surrounded. There's no way you can escape.'

If there had been any doubts at all in the Bavols' minds about the robot's identity, they vanished in that instant. They had given FitzHugh a number four stun; no flesh-and-blood woman would be capable of talking to them now after that. If Elspeth FitzHugh had been a living person, she would still be unconscious for at least an hour. The fact that she had called Pias by his cover name meant she had to have recognized him; only a robot would have reflexes fast enough to notice his face before he'd 'stunned' her.

Despite the grimness of their situation, Pias smiled. 'We Gypsies are old hands at bargaining,' he told Yvette. 'The first rule is, when the other side starts off with a preposterous offer, you make an equally preposterous counter-proposal. You can always work your way down to reality from there.'

Putting the bullhorn to his mouth, he bellowed back, 'I'm afraid that won't do, Sister Elspeth. Instead, I suggest you have your entire army file past the door of the armory and drop their weapons here. Then we can talk.'

There was a short silence from the bottom of the hill. Then FitzHugh's voice came back, 'You know I can't do that.'

'And you know we can't accept your kind offer, either. Shall we begin talking more realistically?'

After another hesitation, FitzHugh said, 'Perhaps we can work out a deal, Brother Cromwell, something to our mutual interests.'

'That sounds a little better. What do you have in mind?'

'First tell my why you came here – and why you broke into our offices in God's Will City.'

Another piece of verification! Only the robot could have identified Pias in that darkened complex. 'I came here to find out why you were trying to kill me,' Pias said. 'Perhaps it's old fashioned of me, but I *was* curious.'

'We weren't trying to kill you.'

'Your man Hoyden told me otherwise.'

Another pause. 'Well, counselor, you must admit that the philosophy you espouse is quite contradictory to our own. Some of our people may have gotten hotheaded in the Lord's cause, but I can assure you they will suffer severe reprimands.'

'Oh good. I was so worried.'

'And now that we've settled that little problem, perhaps you'd care to come out and discuss the rest of our differences in a civilized manner.'

'I'd love to,' Pias replied. 'There's just one more small detail to be taken care of first.'

'What's that?'

'I'd like some assurance that we won't be killed the instant we step outside this building.'

'You have my word as a sister in God that no harm will befall you.'

' "Sister" my *gluteus maximus*,' Yvette growled. 'The only thing *she's* sister to is a B-1014 computer.'

'That's very generous of you,' Pias said via bullhorn. 'But on matters as delicate as this I'm afraid I can't take the word of a second-in-command. I'll have to hear the same vow from Sister Tresa.'

'She's . . . indisposed, as I'm sure you well know.'

'That's smooth, I'm not going anywhere. I can wait. It should only be a couple of hours.'

Pias put down the bullhorn and, despite further entreaties from FitzHugh, did not broadcast another word. Instead, he talked to Yvette about the plans he was developing. 'Now that we know Clunard isn't the robot,' he said, 'we're going to have to take the chance that she's a relatively honest woman who really believes what she says and has been led astray by subtle manipulations from FitzHugh.'

'This may be the biggest gamble of your life,' Yvette said. 'What happens if you're wrong?'

Pias shrugged. 'Then everybody loses.'

CHAPTER FOURTEEN

THE *COMET* GOES TO WORK

Jules and Yvonne had no way to look out of their cargo rocket and see how fast they were moving; the craft had not been intended for passengers, and was not provided with windows. They did know, however, that automated cargo rockets were not renowned for their speed. The rocketbus had made the journey out this far from the base in just under an hour; if the cargo ship took much longer than that getting back, they'd have very little air left to do anything once they got there.

Jules tried to look on the bright side. 'The rocket's much lighter than it normally is, because all it's carrying is us. That should help it move faster.'

With their fate now totally out of their hands for the moment, they sat down in the darkness against the rear wall of the chamber and did their best to conserve their air. They spoke but little, resting instead and trying to make their breaths as shallow as possible. Once they arrived at the base, they knew, they would be involved in more action and would use up oxygen at a prodigious rate. It had to be saved until then.

Jules's feet and ankles were throbbing from where he'd stepped in the molten lead. He experimented a little bit and found that he could stand now if he leaned against something like a wall for support, but that moving at any speed faster than a hobble was impossible. He chafed at the idea of being so helpless, but his wife reminded him that he still had the use of his hands and his mind – potent weapons indeed.

The ride dragged on for agonizing minutes until finally, after an hour, the nose dropped slightly – an indication that their craft was now angling downward toward the base. The DesPlainians checked their air gauges – twenty minutes of oxygen left. With luck, that should just about last them through what they needed to do.

The ship landed with a solid bump, then rolled so that the cargo door was beneath their feet. The d'Alemberts braced themselves for the shock they knew was coming; without warning, the hatch suddenly sprang open, dropping them – slowly, under Slag's light gravity – almost five meters onto the ore stockpile. After a minute, the hatch door closed again and the ship took off, returning to the digging station for another load of ore.

Below them the pile of ore was shifting as it sifted through an opening in the bottom that led almost certainly to a furnace. Overhead, through the open top of the bin in which they were standing, the stars gleamed down out of a jet black sky.

'I think I'd prefer going out that way,' Jules said, pointing upward. There was a ladder along the side wall for inspection parties to get in and out of the bin. Jules pulled himself up the rungs with just the power of his arms, using his legs only to steady himself. Yvonne was right behind him. In a couple of minutes the two SOTE agents were at the rim of the tank, looking down at the base spread out below them.

After scanning the situation for several moments, Jules pointed. 'There,' he said. 'We'll enter through that auxiliary airlock, away from the main occupied section, but we won't take off our suits immediately; I want to be prepared in case they try something desperate, like blowing out a section of the wall to let the air out. If our luck holds there may be some spare tanks at that lock; if not, we work our way around the perimeter of the base to the passenger tube connected to the *Comet*. Once we're safely in there, I don't think they'll be able to hurt us.'

They climbed down the ladder on the outside of the ore bin without anyone spotting them and, as before, Vonnie loaded her husband on her shoulders. She took off at an easy jog across forty meters of open ground before reaching the designated hatch. The airlock was unguarded – after all, there was really no one on Slag against whom to guard it – and they slipped inside without anyone being the wiser. Once inside, they had to move more slowly; the corridors were too low for Vonnie to carry Jules on her back, and he had to hold onto the wall and proceed one slow, painful step at a time.

There were no spare oxygen tanks inside the auxiliary airlock, meaning that they had fourteen minutes to inch their way around the periphery and slip into their own ship – hopefully undetected. Vonnie led the way, blaster drawn, while Jules walked gingerly behind her on his injured feet.

They had traveled three-quarters of the way around to their ship when they encountered a party of workmen coming at them from a cross corridor. The men were curious about these spacesuited figures inside the base, but not immediately hostile. They waved at the pair, and the DesPlainians waved back – but then the workmen noticed the blaster in Vonnie's hand. One of them whispered something to the others, and they suddenly turned and ran back the way they'd come. Vonnie fired a shot and hit one of them in the back of the leg, but the others rounded a corner and were out of sight before she could do anything further.

'The alarm will be raised any second now,' she said. 'This is no time for dignity.'

Picking Jules up bodily, she carried him in her arms like a groom about to carry his new bride across a threshold. She ran at top speed down the empty corridor toward the main reception lock, aware of the precious seconds ticking away. They reached the main lock at almost the same instant as an armed party of their opponents. Vonnie's hands were full, but she trusted Jules to use his blaster effectively enough for the both of them.

Jules did not bother firing at the enemy. Instead, he fired his weapon at the large glass viewing ports that looked out onto the landing field. The glass was reinforced and built to withstand rigorous conditions, but it couldn't hold up to a Mark Twenty-Nine Service blaster's deadly bolts. As it shattered outward, a hurricane hit the reception area.

The force of the air whooshing out of the room nearly pulled Vonnie off her feet, but she managed to brace herself against one wall and hang on until the draft had died down. The enemy forces had not been as lucky. None of them had had time to don their spacesuits, and were unprepared for vacuum conditions. They were ripped off their feet against the forward bulkhead and began gasping for breath that wasn't there. Jules and Yvonne instinctively turned their heads away; they had seen a lot of people die before, but death by explosive decompression was never a pretty sight.

'Have we blown out the whole base?' Vonnie wondered.

'I don't think so. If this is constructed according to standard practice, each doorway is built to shut airtight in case of a blowout. This room will be sealed off from the rest of the base until the blowout can be repaired and internal pressure restored. It'll give us a little time; let's not waste it.'

Yvette steadied herself and opened the door to the passenger tube that led to their own ship. They made it inside, sealed off the tube and turned on the *Comet*'s internal air supply. When the lights told them the air around them was breathable, they cracked open their suits' helmets and breathed the pure, sweet air of the ship – a welcome change after the sweaty environment inside their suits. According to the gauges on their air tanks, they had made it with three minutes to spare.

They had little chance to luxuriate in the fresh oxygen, however. 'We'd better get in to the control room, fast,' Jules said. 'We've still got plenty of work to do.'

Without stopping to remove the rest of his suit, Jules moved over to the ladder and once again began pulling himself up by his arms. He and Yvonne were dead tired after their ordeal on Slag's surface, and both could easily have slept straight through for a week. But there was to be no rest for them yet.

Checking the outside screens, Jules scanned the activity going on around them. The people at the base had reacted far faster to this situation than he had expected; apparently they had practiced invasion drills in case their factory was discovered by imperial forces, and they knew just what they should be doing. Spacesuited figures were running about the field outside, manning the big artillery pieces that had been hidden around the base's perimeter.

Jules realized that, if he was not careful, the *Comet* would be knocked out of the fight while still sitting on the ground – an ignominious defeat for so proud a vessel. Flipping on the series of switches to activate the pile and let the ship warm up, he said, 'We're going to have to get out of here. This fight's far from over.'

Across the field another ship was taking off – Chactan's

ship. 'We can't let him get away,' Vonnie said. 'He has to lead us to his superior.'

'I'll do the best I can,' Jules answered. 'The *Comet*'s a great ship, but she can't take off stone cold.'

The ship rocked from a near miss as one of the big energy guns was swung in its direction. The *Comet* had plenty of offense of its own, but as long as they were sitting here on the ground, Jules couldn't use it. They were inside the weapons' minimum range, and they themselves would be caught in the explosion if they tried to fire back at their attackers. In this particular instance, they suffered from an embarrassment of riches. 'I never thought too much firepower would be a handicap,' Jules muttered.

The board suddenly gave him a green, and Jules did not hesitate. Slapping at his switches, he goosed the ship to maximum power and the *Copper Comet* leaped off the surface of Slag at the devastating acceleration of fifteen gees, crushing its two inhabitants into their acceleration couches. All around them, more energy bolts exploded, some perilously near – but none of the enemy gunners had expected the *Comet* to rise quite that quickly and their aim was affected by their miscalculations.

After several seconds of the intense acceleration, Jules reached out a heavy hand to shut it off and the pair suddenly found themselves in freefall. Had Slag been a world with an atmosphere Jules would have waited longer to clear it; the *Comet* had not been designed with intricate atmospheric maneuvering in mind. It was a space fighter, as out of place in open air as a fish.

But the vacuum above Slag gave Jules the perfect opportunity to slew the ship around and point the weapons downward at the base below. As he gripped the controls he tried not to think of the two thousand individual lives down there; they were all just the enemy, and they were more than willing to do the same to him.

The *Comet*'s guns spoke, with all the authority SOTE had built into them. For a moment, the base down on the surface was enveloped in a red glow, an almost peaceful sight in contrast to the hell the d'Alemberts knew it truly was. If the base had been of a more ordinary nature, it simply would have blown apart under the ferocious energies focused on it;

but being a manufacturing plant for highly explosive materials, the d'Alemberts' blast triggered a chain reaction within the base itself. With the silent suddenness of events in a vacuum, the entire base vaporized in a fireball of blinding intensity. Jules and Yvonne could not keep their eyes on the screen, and when the glow had died all that was left of the base was yet another crater on the face of Slag.

Jules sighed and turned the ship outward once more. 'Now, let's go after Chactan,' he said grimly.

The other man's ship had only a couple minutes' head start, and could not compare in speed to the *Copper Comet*. Had Jules opened his ship to the limit, he could easily have overtaken the fugitive and either blown it apart or forced it to surrender. But that was not his intent now. He had theorized while traveling across the surface of Slag that Chactan had some high-level help on Tregania itself; now that the man was fleeing for his life, he would certainly head for the nearest and strongest place of refuge – and the d'Alemberts were only too willing to let him get there. That would save them a lot of time and investigative effort.

Jules therefore was careful to match his speed almost exactly to that of his quarry, allowing his ship to close the gap at an excruciating pace. As they'd figured, Chactan's ship did not dive into subspace the instant it was beyond the safety limit of Slag's gravitational field, but instead headed straight for the inhabited planet of this system, Tregania, which was presently one quarter of the way around the sun from Slag and millions of kilometers further out.

The ship's computer informed them that, at present speeds, it would take them better than twelve hours to reach the other world – time which the d'Alemberts could put to good use. Jules radioed ahead on the standard SOTE frequency to the Service headquarters on Tregania. His code name, Wombat, got him quickly through to the local chief, a man named Lee. Jules explained the situation succinctly and Lee nodded. 'My entire office is at your disposal,' Lee said when Jules had finished, 'but I'm afraid that's not as much as either of us would like. Tregania's always been a quiet place, and the Service only has a few ships stationed here. I'll put through a priority call to the Navy, but it'll take them at least a day, possibly longer, to arrive.'

Jules nodded grimly, then began giving his instructions. Lee was to put all the ships he had aloft, but keep them as inconspicuous as possible. He gave them the course coordinates of Chactan's ship, but warned that under no circumstances was Chactan to be interfered with until he reached his destination. Once he had landed and joined with his allies, there would be no holds barred. The penalty for treason, after all, was death. It was hoped, though, that they could take the leaders alive to question them about possible connections to any conspiracies higher up.

That accomplished, Jules and Yvonne could take care of more pressing bodily needs. Both were famished and both were fatigued; in addition, Jules's feet were still throbbing from the burns they'd received. They were finally able to doff their spacesuits – Jules with some difficulty because of the solidified lead coating on his boots – and Vonnie rubbed some first-aid cream on Jules's blistering feet before floating back to the ship's compact galley to fix them a quick, nourishing snack. When they had both eaten, Jules insisted that Vonnie sleep for the first five-hour shift; she had done most of the work carrying him across the plains of Slag, and she was the most tired. His wife gave him little argument. When the shift was over, Jules woke her and she stood watch over the instruments while Jules had some rest of his own. Vonnie was not as good a pilot as her husband; her primary duty was to make sure Chactan kept to his previous course without trying any new tricks. If something out of the ordinary were to occur, she was to wake Jules instantly.

Chactan's only concern, though, seemed to be escaping from his pursuers, and he strove for that goal with single-minded determination. When Vonnie woke Jules half an hour out from Tregania, Chactan's ship was still on the same desperate trajectory and the *Comet* was only marginally closer.

'Time to really turn the screws,' Jules said as he strapped himself down once again in front of the control console. He and Yvonne were now feeling rested from their ordeal on Slag, and were actually looking forward to the upcoming battle with a great deal of relish. They had spent weeks on this case so far, and were eager for its conclusion.

At his deft command, the *Comet* suddenly leaped ahead

toward the ship it was chasing. It must have come as a shock to the occupants of the other craft to see the ship that had been just matching their speed for so many hours start to close the gap with ease. Their vessel was already traveling at its top speed; there was no way they could outdistance their pursuer now.

'Do you think it would scare them a little more if I fired at them?' Jules wondered aloud.

'I think we can save our guns for better effect,' Vonnie replied. 'I traveled from Nampur to Slag on that ship, and I took the chance to look around. It's just a passenger ship, no armament of any kind except a few handguns. If we shot at them they might just stop dead, and we'd lose the connection. We want to tickle them a little, not scare them to death.'

'*Khorosho*,' Jules agreed. 'No shooting, we just push them a little harder.'

But as the *Comet* gained on its prey it soon became clear that Jules was not the only person who had radioed ahead to Tregania for help. A fleet of seven ships rose from the planet, racing upward toward a meeting with Chactan's craft. 'I told Lee to remain inconspicuous,' Jules muttered. 'Those can't be his ships.'

Indeed they weren't. As they drew nearer to the pair of ships from Slag, it was obvious they were going to let the first go by them. Their target was the *Comet* – and there could be little doubt that these ships *were* armed. 'Better start evading,' Vonnie said – but even as she opened her mouth, Jules was playing with his controls, maneuvering their ship into position for a fight against vastly greater odds. Yvonne, meanwhile, turned for the radio and started calling Lee, telling him that the time for subtlety had passed.

A stream of tiny blips on the screens showed a pattern of space torpedoes laid down in their path by the seven oncoming cruisers. Jules turned on the rapidfire autoblasters. The sensors locked onto the targets and a series of small staccato bursts of energy blazed forth from positions around the *Comet*'s hull. Directly ahead a series of silent explosions meant that the autoblasters had done their job, clearing a path through the torpedo field. Jules's concentration was entirely on the space ahead as he steered the vessel through the lane it had opened up.

Beside him, Vonnie had finished talking to Lee and was busy at her own task – manning the *Comet*'s not inconsiderable offensive array. Those seven enemy cruisers might have them outnumbered, but they'd learn that dealing with d'Alemberts meant they were in for a fight.

Her job as gunner was complicated by the fact that Jules was twisting the ship around constantly to avoid the enemy's weapons. Yvette, having worked with her brother for years, could have formed an almost telepathic rapport with him, knowing instinctively which way he would go and being able to compensate for it in her aim. Yvonne, having teamed with Jules for a shorter time, was less sure what he would do under any given circumstance, and her aim suffered slightly because of it. Even so, her shots were landing close enough to the enemy ships that they had to take some evasive action of their own, easing a little of the pressure on Jules.

Then suddenly the attack ceased completely as five SOTE fighters zoomed into view from out of nowhere and the enemy cruisers changed course to face this new threat. One of them swung directly into Vonnie's crosshairs, and she blasted it to shards of glowing debris with evident satisfaction.

'Forget them,' Jules told his wife. 'Chactan's getting away, and he's the one we really want. Lee can handle these *mokoes* in his own.'

Ignoring the fighting, then, the *Copper Comet* flashed through the battle zone and followed doggedly after the quarry it had already chased a quarter of the way around this solar system. Chactan's ship dipped into the atmosphere and began the complex downward spiral of a landing pattern. Jules was tracking it every second, and laid the coordinates of the orbit into the ship's computer to tell him where the other vessel was going to set down. The computer translated the numbers into a location on the planetary grid and, since the spot was on the hemisphere of Tregania facing the ship, it locked its telescopic cameras on the site.

The picture that appeared on the central screen made both agents gasp. It was a fortress whose thick walls must have encompassed fifty hectares. The main building was a group of four connected towers, massive stone cylinders rising twenty stories into the air. Beside the grouping was a private spaceport field – from which, no doubt, the seven attack ships had been launched and to which Chactan was now speeding. Scattered around the grounds were ominous lumps; a casual observer might have thought they were intended as unusual art forms or whimsies on the part of the estate's owner, but to Jules's trained eye they looked suspiciously like heavy gun emplacements.

'Someone was expecting a fight when he designed that place,' Jules said.

'Your assumption was right,' Vonnie acknowledged. 'It's the Duke himself – no one of lesser importance could command a fort that imposing.'

'We'll have to shift tactics. The *Comet* isn't really built for atmospheric maneuvering, and if we try to land where Chactan's going we'll be blown to a powder so thin they couldn't hold us in a sieve.'

As he spoke, Jules was taking the big ship down to the upper reaches of Tregania's atmosphere and setting it on autopilot to maintain an orbit at that altitude. He and Yvonne then went aft to the chamber where their aircar, the Mark Forty-One Service special, was snugged in its special niche. They turned on the internal systems and locked the protective bubble around the car, making it airtight. Then, at a command from the car's control console, the *Comet* opened the bay hatch and the tiny car pushed itself away from the ship, downward toward the surface of Tregania.

The fall was in reality a carefully controlled glide, with Jules monitoring their progress every meter of the way. He was aiming to bring the car down near the fortress, just a short distance outside the walls. 'They don't know about this car yet,' he explained to Vonnie, 'but if we come down right on top of them they'll blow us out of the sky just for target practice. Those big guns are aimed to defend against attack from the sky. If we come in low, the guns will be useless.'

They watched on their screens as Chactan's ship set down on the spacefield and its occupants ran for cover inside the fortress towers. It took only another five minutes before they themselves were down, a kilometer north of the wall. Jules kept them hovering just a few meters above ground level while he and Vonnie checked to see that all their armaments were in good working order. When the final light on the board flashed a welcome green, Jules gave his wife a brief nod. 'Hang onto your hair,' he said. 'We're going in.'

The little car accelerated straight ahead at a rate of nearly five gees. The wall came up to meet them at a breathtaking rate, but the touch of a button from Yvonne caused a high intensity beam to lash out and demolish a section of the barrier in front of them. They zipped *through* the wall and into the grounds beyond.

As they passed the towers the first time, Vonnie gave them several strong bolts from her heavy duty multiblasters. The towers shook, but remained standing; the stonework on the outside must have been ornamental, concealing some sturdy shielding underneath. The car raced past before she had time for more than one salvo, but there was no hurry. There were plenty of other targets deserving her attentions, and the towers would still be there the next time they came around in that direction.

Jules had memorized the layout of the grounds as he'd studied it from the air, and had planned his route with clinical precision. He headed for the first of the gun emplacements at a speed so great that the defenders could not keep up with him. Even had the gun been built to deal with a menace charging at it from ground level, its operators still would have been reluctant to fire for fear of missing the car and hitting the towers instead. The fortress was armed with an elephant gun and was trying to stop a wasp.

The d'Alemberts displayed no reluctance whatsoever at showing their sting. Jules was taking their vehicle on a wide swing around the emplacement, giving Vonnie plenty of time to perfect her marksmanship. He needn't have bothered; one shot was all his wife needed. In a matter of seconds the big gun outside was just a towering column of flames and black smoke and the pesky aircar was on its way to the second target.

The fort's defender tried gamely to stop the invaders from SOTE, but their attempts fell pitifully short. Most of the stronghold's defense had been centered around the big weapons, capable of stopping any attack from space. The defenders scattered about the grounds had only handheld blasters, not at all sufficient for penetrating the shields that surrounded the d'Alembert vehicle.

Jules ignored the ground fire and concentrated exclusively on knocking out the big weapons. One by one they fell as Vonnie maintained a perfect shooting record. Jules would chide her later that they had all been easy sitting targets, but at the time they were only concerned that the job be done right. As the last of the emplacements was destroyed, Jules lifted the aircar off the ground and took it in a leisurely flight around the four grouped towers that constituted the main building.

The defenders tried some last-ditch shooting, but the SOTE vehicle's shields had been designed to withstand far worse. As Jules made lazy circles around the towers like a hawk, Vonnie dropped a series of bombs that shook the ground beneath them and caused part of one tower to crumble away.

The radio crackled to life over the standard SOTE frequency. 'Wombat, this is Lee. We've taken care of the problem upstairs and we're coming down with three ships – if you need them.'

At the same time, Vonnie pointed to the car's screens. Someone was raising a white flag atop one of the towers. The DesPlainians slumped back in their chairs with evident relief.

They hovered in their car over the scene, watching casually as Lee's ships landed and took charge. The fortress's defenders were led out at gunpoint, and would all be taken to local headquarters for intensive questioning.

Jules would also be visiting the local headquarters to have a Service doctor check out his burned feet and start them on the road to recovery. But the d'Alemberts' active role was about at an end. After giving Lee a briefing on what questions to ask, they could at last return home to DesPlaines.

CHAPTER FIFTEEN

THE DUEL ON THE HILL

Back on Purity, the situation remained tense. Despite repeated pleas from FitzHugh, the Bavols refused to speak further until Tresa Clunard could be roused from the stun charge they had given her.

Most of the time Pias took on the dull job of holding the cord of the dead man's switch. Yvette rested, but with gun at the ready. Her left shoulder was still aching, but she bore up well and only by looking closely could Pias tell the pain she was under.

During one brief shift while Yvette relieved him at the cord, Pias looked over the armory and catalogued its contents. Not only were there plenty of handweapons, but also the large heavy duty models on their mobile tripods. There were cases of explosives and box after box of the acid-mix fuses needed to set them off. There were rows and rows of heavy body armor for use in space battles. Pias took thoughtful note of all these things, then returned to his post and relieved Yvette of the cord once more.

Finally, after what seemed like an eternity, a new voice came booming up the hill at them. 'This is Tresa Clunard. I understand you want to talk to me.'

Pias took up the bullhorn again. 'Yes indeed. You're going to find this a little difficult to believe, Sister Tresa, but we mean you no personal harm.'

'You *do* have an odd way of demonstrating such intentions.'

'We could have killed you back in your office if we'd wished. We'd hoped to avoid senseless killing. We still do, as a matter of fact. We are here to warn you of a traitor in your midst.'

'Why should you do that for me?'

'Sister Tresa, we have both worked as servants of God. I grant you that our theological stances have been far apart –

some might even say diametrically opposed – but I'm sure even you will have to admit that at no time did I ever counsel anyone to go against God's will. We have different interpretations of that will, but will you at least admit that I am sincerely on the side of God?'

'You seem to be.' Clunard was still defensive.

'Then I say to you, as someone who loves God as dearly as you do, that there is in your organization a traitor not only to you, but to me, to Purity, and all of Mankind. This person has joined your movement only to subvert it, to twist its goals around to her own secular purposes. She would use the force that you have built up, not for fighting God's battle, but for fighting the battles of her treasonous masters. She is using you shamelessly for unholy ends, and she herself is a slave to the very machines you decry so loudly.'

He paused for breath, and Yvette took the opportunity to ask him, 'Aren't you going to say she *is* a machine?'

'Never tell an audience more than they're prepared to believe,' Pias said in an aside to his wife. 'Clunard will have a hard enough time believing FitzHugh's a traitor; if I said she was a robot as well, my entire story would be discredited.'

His remarks to Yvette made the pause longer than he had intended, and Clunard took the opportunity to interject a question of her own. 'Whom do you accuse in my army?'

Pias took a deep breath. 'I accuse Elspeth FitzHugh of being a traitor to you, to the Empire and to God Himself.'

Down the hill there was a brief moment of stunned silence. 'There is no one in the Universe more loyal to me than Sister Elspeth,' Clunard said at last.

'Or no one who pretends to be,' Pias countered.

'What evidence can you offer of her treason?'

'I have no physical evidence. I have investigated the matter thoroughly, however, and all the evidence is inescapable.'

'Your theology is faulty, why should I expect that your deductive powers are any better?'

'Because we are at an impasse, Sister Tresa. You were wondering how it could be broken, and I've just told you. Deliver Elspeth FitzHugh to us and we will leave quietly. We want nothing more from you.'

'I'd sooner give up my right arm,' Clunard shot back.

Pias did not respond, and silence settled over the camp for several minutes. 'Brother Cromwell?' Clunard called again.

'Yes?'

'Sister Elspeth has made a suggestion. Personally, I find your entire argument ludicrous and without foundation, but she insists on treating it seriously. Her honor has been besmirched, and she seeks the opportunity to right it again in the eyes of God and of men.'

'How does she propose to do that?'

'A duel. You and she will battle, alone and unarmed, in front of all of us. If you win, you will have what you say you want, and you will leave us in peace. If she wins, you will no longer be a threat to us and we will trust your wife to surrender as well.'

'I thought trial by combat went out with the Inquisition,' Pias muttered under his breath.

As though reading his thoughts, Clunard continued, 'I've told Sister Elspeth that I didn't want to risk her in such a foolish endeavor, but such is her faith that she knows God will give her the strength she needs, just as He gives me the strength to bend the metal rods.'

'*Khorosho*, I accept,' Pias said.

Yvette looked at him wide-eyed. 'Are you crazy? Fitz-Hugh would never have suggested that if she thought there was a chance she could lose. She's a robot, remember – stronger, faster and with better reflexes. In unarmed combat you don't stand a chance against her.'

'She can't use her full strength or her full speed against me,' Pias replied calmly. 'Even these people's belief in miracles can only extend so far. If she looks too superhuman they may begin to wonder – and remember how paranoid these robots are about giving themselves away.'

'She doesn't have to go full out. All she has to do is be a split second faster, a tiny bit stronger. One sharp blow to the neck can kill without appearing to be hocus-pocus.'

Pias flashed her a confident smile. 'We Gypsies have a few fighting tricks of our own. I'll be careful.'

A few moments later, Pias appeared at the door to the arsenal, looking down on the assembled army – and at Clunard and FitzHugh. 'I'm alone and unarmed,' he called, spreading his arms to show that he carried no weapons. 'My wife is back inside there, still holding the cord. If there is any treachery against me, she'll drop it instantly.'

'What about you?' FitzHugh asked. 'Will you stand by the agreement if you lose?'

'I swear by almighty God that I will,' Pias said. 'And my wife has assured me that she will, too. But if you break your word and use any artificial weapons, then the deal is off and I'll defend myself as I choose.'

'Agreed,' Clunard said before FitzHugh could advise her differently.

The robot stepped forward. Her back was to Clunard and to the army, but Pias could detect the hint of a smile at the edges of her lips. She knew that on this three gravity planet there was no one stronger or faster than she was. And if her opponent should pull a weapon, she could still react fast enough to dodge it – plus, it would brand him a liar and a cheat.

Pias stood his ground in a slight crouch. The snow underfoot had been trampled and was becoming a bit slushy. For the moment he held a slight advantage; FitzHugh had to come uphill to approach him. But that advantage would not last long; if his plan was to succeed, he would have to intentionally give up the edge, turn her around so that she was facing the troops and Tresa Clunard down below.

FitzHugh approached with the easy confidence of a sure winner, while Pias held his body tense and ready to spring. Yvette had been right about one thing: he dared not let the robot get in so much as a single solid blow, or he was doomed. Even if she didn't kill him outright, one quick strike would disable him enough to let her finish at her leisure. He had to win without touching her; and despite his confidence in front of Yvette, there were some doubts in the back of his mind that he could manage it.

She came within two meters of him and stopped. For more than a minute the two antagonists faced one another, neither moving. *I don't have to make the first move*, Pias told himself. *Let her do all the work.*

Tiring at last of the deadlock, FitzHugh feinted with her left shoulder and started toward Pias on her right foot. The SOTE agent held his ground as long as possible to make sure there were no double-feints, then at the last instant danced out of the way of the charge. The robot raced past, reaching out as she went by and just missing with a grab for Pias's shirt. The SOTE agent thought the other's momentum would carry her several metres past him, but she was able to spin around in the snow faster than he expected and make another lunge at him. He was able to avoid this one only by the ungraceful expedient of sliding to the ground. He scrambled to his feet quickly after she'd passed, reminding himself not to underestimate her abilities.

'What's the matter, Brother Cromwell?' FitzHugh taunted. 'Has your God suddenly deserted you?'

Pias did not bother to reply. The robot could afford to talk; it didn't need air to live. Pias preferred to save his breath for the action that was to come.

The robot made three more charges, and each time Pias was able to duck out of the way – but his margin for error grew smaller with each pass. Pias's native planet, Newforest, had a surface gravity of two and a half gees, while here on Purity the gravity was three gees. Under normal circumstances the difference was not significant – but in a stressful situation such as this, that extra half gee could make a considerable difference. Pias was tiring a trifle more easily than he should. He knew he would have to make his move soon, or the robot might get its chance to kill him before he could play out his trick.

He maneuvered himself into position to make it work. All during the fight he had been edging his way down the hillside, closer to Clunard and the army. He wanted to make sure they would have a good view of what was about to transpire. He was now as close as he could hope for. The robot was downhill from him, preparing for another charge upward. In the past, it had always gone past him, pivoted and made a charge back down the hill at him; he prayed it would continue in that pattern one more time.

As he waited, he shook his right sleeve slightly, letting the tiny vial he had concealed there slip down into his hand. It was a container of acid from one of the acid-mix fuses in the armory. Pias felt justified in using it despite his promise because, after all, the robot had attacked him with something artificial – itself. He would have only the one chance to throw it, though, so he had to do it well; he needed to hit a spot where there was plenty of 'skin' rather than clothing.

FitzHugh charged and Pias stepped aside to avoid the rush once more, simultaneously flinging the bottle into the robot's face. The thin glass shattered, spilling the acid over the automaton's visage, even as she whirled to make another downhill pass.

Pias had not stood his ground this time, but had run several steps further downhill toward Clunard and the army. 'I want you to look carefully, Sister Tresa,' he shouted. 'Look at this *thing* you trust so deeply.'

The acid had begun to eat quickly away at FitzHugh's artificial skin, revealing the machinery behind it. The robot froze, aware it was being exposed but uncertain, for a split second, how to deal with the situation. In the meantime Tresa Clunard and her Army of the Just had a clear view at the workings behind FitzHugh's face.

'It's a machine, Sister Tresa,' Pias continued, hammering his point home. 'You have been fooled by the very machines you claim to detest. You have listened to their advice and trusted them, and they have betrayed you and misled you. *That* machine is your enemy, not I.'

The FitzHugh robot, realizing it was useless now in its undercover role, began to flee up the hill, moving at a speed no human being could have matched. It had gone only a few dozen meters, though, when a blaster bolt sizzled out of the armory, hitting it squarely in the chest. Yvette's shot knocked the robot to the ground. The machine sputtered for a moment, twitched its limbs a few times and then lay still.

Silence blanketed the hillside for half a minute. Then a few bold members of the army detached themselves from the group and went over to inspect the corpse. The blaster bolt had laid open the robot even further, and its workings were self-evident. The soldiers looked down at FitzHugh and then over to Tresa Clunard. There was a new expression on their faces. Before this moment, Tresa Clunard had been, if not a demigod, then at least a saint. But now, to see that she had been fooled so badly by a symbol of all she had preached was evil, their adoration was fading rapidly.

Pias fought to hold back a smile. *There are some people*

who'll stay with her no matter what, he thought. *But by nightfall I doubt she'll have more than a few hundred followers in her army.* The threat from this paramilitary force had been ended.

He and Clunard stared at one another for a moment, both aware of the momentous change that had occurred. There didn't seem to be much left to say to one another so, with a shrug, Pias turned his back and began walking back up the hill to the armory.

'Brother Cromwell,' she called, and Pias turned. 'Are you satisfied now that you've destroyed me?'

'That was never my intention,' he said gently. 'I merely wanted to show you the error of your ways. We can all get so caught up in our causes that we lose sight of the morality of the situation.'

'I still believe I'm right,' she said. 'I will continue exhorting against decadence in society.'

'I never asked you to stop.' And Pias climbed uphill once more to help Yvette dismantle the dead man's switch. As he reached the armory he looked back. Clunard was on her knees beside the body of the FitzHugh robot. She was praying – but what she was praying for, he never learned.

CHAPTER SIXTEEN

PROBLEMS AHEAD

As Pias had suspected, the Army of the Just virtually disintegrated during that day. Their respect for Tresa Clunard had shattered along with the robot and, while they might still agree with her philosophy, they simply could not follow her as a military leader after she had been so badly duped by the enemy. True to Clunard's promise, Pias and Yvette were allowed to leave in peace. They made it back to their aircar and called the local SOTE headquarters, explaining what had happened.

When the regular SOTE forces arrived at the camp they met with no active resistance. Most of the volunteers were in the process of leaving, and SOTE didn't try to stop them. The weapons in the armory were confiscated, and the camp's buildings were burned. Tresa Clunard was taken into temporary custody and given a stern lecture on loyalty to the Empire. She listened sullenly and gave her word never to organize a military force against the lawfully constituted government again. The local SOTE chief, seeing no point in detaining her further, merely suspended her counseling license for five years and released her.

Two days later, a regularly scheduled flight departed from Purity to DesPlaines. On board were two very tired and very satisfied SOTE agents. Yvette had had her shoulder wound treated by a Service doctor, and had received assurances she would be fit as new in a week or two.

'In a way,' she said to her husband during the flight, 'I feel a little sorry for Clunard. There she was at the peak of her persuasive powers, an army of ten thousand people at her command, knowing with absolute certainty that God was on her side, and then it all crashed down around her in a matter of seconds.'

'Pity is the last thing you should feel for her,' Pias remarked. 'She'll bounce back; fanatics always do. In some ways, this might be the best thing that could have happened to her. Fanatics are really at their best when they're the underdogs. If they ever get into a position where they're in charge, everyone's in trouble. As long as Tresa Clunard is kept out of any positions of real power, everything will be smooth.'

The trip back to DesPlaines proved uneventful. The Bavols found themselves greeted at the spaceport by Jules and Yvonne, who had beaten them home by two days. There was a happy reunion and a great deal of backslapping, as each team was relieved to see that the other had survived its mission. As they drove back to the ducal mansion, *Felicité*, they exchanged stories about how their tasks had gone, and each tried to make their own adventures sound more harrowing than the other's.

When they arrived at the estate, Jules and Yvette parted temporarily from their respective spouses and went straight to the communications room to report in person to the Head. It happened to be nighttime at the Head's home on Earth, but he was always willing to be awakened with good news from his two best agents. Jules had already made his report two days ago, and Yvette boiled hers down so concisely that it took only ten minutes. A more detailed written report, of course, would follow.

The Head, as always, listened attentively. 'That's one less robot to worry about,' he remarked when Yvette had finished. 'But there's still at least one more somewhere – and your supposition, Yvette, that the robots take subordinate roles coincides with my own theory. But that only makes the remaining robot, or robots, harder to find. A male from a heavy-grav planet ...' His voice trailed off as he looked thoughtful.

'Did you get my message from Purity and check out my hunch?' Yvette asked, since the conversation had drifted this way.

'Yes, I did. Sorry, but for once you're wrong; our chief on Newforest was able to do a quick test unnoticed on Pias's brother. Tas Bavol is not a robot. Whatever mischief he may be up to, it's purely human mischief.' He saw Yvette's face fall, and continued quickly, 'That's not to underestimate it, of course; human mischief is the worst kind. It's usually more inventive. I don't approve of the younger Lord Bavol's actions myself, and I've ordered the chief there to keep a watchful eye on things. But for the moment there's little we can do until he actually makes his move.'

Their boss changed his expression once again as he glanced over toward Jules. 'There've been more developments on your case since I last spoke to you. Duke Morro of Tregania has been talking so fast we can hardly keep up with him. He doesn't know Lady A, claims never to have heard of her, and since the rest of his story checks out I tend to believe him. He does confirm some of what we know about the mysterious C, though. He's never met C, nor does he know of anyone who has. All of C's messages come over the telecom circuit, written out on the screen. If a physical copy is required, it's burned the instant it's served its purpose. There is never anything left to give any clues to C's identity or whereabouts.'

'Just what we needed,' Jules said, grimacing. 'We only started getting a handle on Lady A when someone else came along. If he never goes anywhere and only communicates via telecom, he could be sitting on any planet in the Empire and there's no way to track him back.'

'I suspect he must be Lady A's superior,' Yvette said, thinking aloud. 'He stays quietly at home, running the show. If there are any errands to be run, he lets her do them. That way she faces all the risks, he's still safe.' The thought of anyone who could boss the awesome Lady A around was frightening indeed, but the conclusion made sense to Yvette.

The Head nodded slowly. 'Your thinking matches my own – which makes the capture of Lady A even more necessary. She's probably the only person who will be able to tell us the identity of C.'

'And finding her won't be easy, either,' Jules said. 'We've been so close a couple of times – but close doesn't get us any points.'

'There's going to be more pressure on us in the upcoming weeks than ever before,' the Head continued. 'I want you both on standby alert for instant action. Four days from now, the Emperor is going on a Galaxy-wide com network to make a major announcement. He's going to be abdicating on his seventieth birthday in favor of Edna.'

Neither Jules nor Yvette was particularly surprised. Although the timing of the event was, to their minds, premature – William Stanley was still a healthy and capable man – the fact of his abdication had been discussed in their very first meeting with him. 'I'm sorry to see it happen so soon,' Jules said. 'I don't think I've ever met anyone so ideally suited for the position.'

'With the possible exception of Edna,' Yvette smiled. 'And it's not as if he'll be dead and buried; he'll still be around to give counsel and guidance for a long time to come. It's just that he'll have a little more time to enjoy life without the press of responsibilities.'

'There is the precedent for this timing, too,' their boss reminded them. 'If you remember your history, Empress Stanley Three abdicated in favor of her son Karl when she was seventy, so Bill decided that was as good a deadline for him as any. But that's only a few months away, and you can bet that if Lady A and her crew had something special in mind for Edna's wedding they'll make an even more concerted effort around the time of the coronation. A government is always at its most vulnerable when there's a transition of power from one person to another. I have a feeling Edna is going to get her baptism of fire very shortly after ascending the Throne – and it'll be up to us to ensure that she survives it.'

And, elsewhere in the Galaxy, Lady A – having spent a few hours cursing SOTE's interference in her plans – calmly turned her devious mind to the next operation . . .